The Rose Quartz
ARROWHEAD

The Rose Quartz
ARROWHEAD

The Land Beneath Our Feet

JANICE CREEL CLARK

Archway Publishing books may be ordered through booksellers or by contacting:

Archway Publishing
1663 Liberty Drive
Bloomington, IN 47403
www.archwaypublishing.com
844-669-3957

Interior Image Credit: From the author's photo collection

ISBN: 978-1-6657-3227-7 (sc)
ISBN: 978-1-6657-3228-4 (e)

Library of Congress Control Number: 2022919699

Print information available on the last page.

Archway Publishing rev. date: 01/26/2023

CONTENTS

DEDICATION

- To the Harkness women of every generation
- To volunteers at historical societies throughout the state of Alabama
- In loving memory of my aunt, Annie Creel Adams (1903–2002)

PREFACE

Untold stories lie just beneath the feet of Alabamians today, whether they are standing in their front lawns in spacious wooded subdivisions or walking from concrete parking lots into big box stores in retail shopping centers.

According to William Alexander Read's 1934 book *Indian Place Names in Alabama*, over five hundred cities, towns, and small settlements have been known by their Native American names. I chose one that vanished when the site was captured and destroyed in 1813. In this novel, the hamlet's name, Littafuchee, is borrowed from an ancient site in Saint Clair County whose meaning is "those who make arrows straight" or "those who shoot with straight arrows."

Like Native American children, my children were part of the forests, creeks, and rocky soil that no one wanted until the highway system came through. As sheltered as my children were growing up in this beautiful place, they observed and experienced enough of what's not pretty about segregation and gun violence, among other realities. I did my best to show them what a life lived with integrity could be as this city girl adapted to life in an all-white farming community on the verge of joining the twentieth century.

We moved away, returning in 2014 to a rural South conveniently connected in all directions to modern, industrialized metropolitan centers. Fast foods, retail opportunities, and outpatient medical facilities were minutes away. Homes with acreage were affordable.

A diversity of newcomers whose jobs transferred them to Alabama were residents. Internationals who attended our state's fine universities and then stayed on to teach and work in medical facilities or in the auto or aerospace industries now populate the rural areas with us.

In our subdivision, deer sleep on a knoll behind our house at the dark edge of the streetlight's glow. Woodland critters visit our back porch at night curiously peering into low windows at the digital TV's glow inside. Birds and chipmunks wait for sunrise to take their places. Both native and landscaped flowers bloom in my yard year around thanks to hardy camellias and yellow forsythias fooled by warm winter sun in central Alabama.

My grandchildren learn daily from their classmates who are minorities, immigrants, bilingual, and whose families practice religions and observe celebrations unlike ours. What an interesting time to be a student in Alabama!

Yes, change has come to rural Alabama. What I write about are the "whispers," the rural experiences of deep meaning to folks who've lived on the land and who know their own family stories. During their youth, rural children swam in creeks, picnicked in cemeteries certain Sundays, and collected arrowheads in freshly plowed fields. They got cockleburs in their hair playing in corn fields and deep woods, drank dippers of cold well water from buckets, and warmed in winter by wood-burning stoves. Many worked long hours alongside adults on family-owned farms.

Historical events alluded to throughout the novel are used as storytelling pieces as perceived by the fictional characters. Scholarly histories of Alabama are available at bookstores and online. Local histories are recorded by historical societies.

If you are an older teen, learn about the lives of the people living in Alabama forty years ago. If you lived it, recall those little whispers, rarely mentioned these days.

The Rose Quartz Arrowhead starts where it should with recognition of the indigenous inhabitants who lived on the land thousands of years before us, called Native Americans. It weaves the stories of four young women over time, each in possession of the ornamental arrowhead.

—Janice Creel Clark
January 2022

ACKNOWLEDGMENT

Cover art by Robbie Clark, *Liquid Landscape*, 2020, used with permission.

PROLOGUE

Princess Half-Moon, a Short Story
By Anne Beatrice, Age sixteen, year 1919

"To understand the mountain, begin by knowing the soil," Half-Moon's grandmother had told her often as they tilled their patch of fertile riverbank near the Creek Indian village.

In the spring, with crude tools in hand, the women and girls turned the soil near their wooden huts to plant maize and other vegetables.

The men did not help often in family gardens, pulling weeds and watering the young plants until they were strong enough to survive the hot summer sun. Instead, strong men cultivated fields of large-kernel corn and hunted game. Old men taught young men to knap arrowheads for hunting from flint rocks and to lash them onto shafts with thin leather strips.

The other warriors from the Muscogee confederacy of other Creeks, Cherokee, and Chickasaw admired the perfectly straight arrows made by the warriors from the foothills' village.

"To understand where the river goes, ask the hawk," Half-Moon's grandfather replied once when she complained that, as a female, she could not go on hunting expeditions with the hunters.

She had never traveled farther along the mountain range than the annual journey with her family, members of the priestly Clan of the Wind, to the wide cave whenever the wise elders decided it was necessary to take winter shelter.

There they would all huddle around fires where men told stories of brave warriors, past and present. They praised the most legendary of them all, Red Eagle, who had been their leader.

Half-Moon wanted to see what was beyond the mountain in all directions, especially where the hunters said a broad river was pulled toward the setting sun. She had seen how other waters rushed southwest, propelled by rocky waterfalls and frequent mergers that followed the hills and valleys with an urgency that rarely slowed and never stopped. She was curious whether they ever ended.

The girl wanted to know and see many things. However, she was to be wed at the end of the Green Corn Harvest to the medicine man's son, Yellow Leaf.

By next summer, the clan would expect her to deliver a first baby. They would expect more after that when they left this land to go to a place out west called Oklahoma where they had been guaranteed new land with no white encroachers. Either way, soon the young wife would experience trudging busy trails in a strange land and crossing bodies of water while carrying a baby strapped to her. They would subsist on few rations and the wild nuts and sweet berries she could gather along the way.

But today, characteristically, Half-Moon had wandered away from the other women and children cultivating their plots of land. This time her feet stepped swiftly across a log, over the stream, along narrow deer trails near the base, and up to the mountain's bald, ragged face. The physical striations from eons of rain had etched long tears down the rock face.

Her left arm wrapped securely around her woven willow basket full of yams. Her fingers dug into crevices as she searched for handholds along the sheer cliff. Although it had been four seasons since she had walked with the stoic procession to bury her grandfather, a tribal elder, she remembered the way.

About halfway up the canyon wall was a wide natural ledge where the Clan of the Wind buried the bodies of their highest-ranking leaders and warriors. Her grandfather's bones were there.

Storytellers said he had been a strong, fearless Red Stick warrior alongside Red Eagle, who was a convincing orator as well as fighter. Red Eagle and the prophets who had traveled with him had told the villages' warriors they would always be victorious in their battles with the white settlers.

Because Red Eagle's words were considered sacred, all the warriors of her clan and from nearby villages went into the battle at Tohopeka assured of success. It had cost so many Red Sticks' lives there were not enough warriors left to continue fighting.

For some compelling reason, Half-Moon felt the need to be near the spirit of her grandfather. Perhaps he had answers to the many questions she had asked of the others regarding the long journey they all were to take.

She glanced over her shoulder and paused before going farther.

A mottled brown hawk hovered overhead, drifting in the air current. His wing tips looked like fingers pointing up, then down, in a come-hither gesture.

It was then she realized the hawk was her grandfather's spirit watching over her!

"Grandfather, it's me," Half-Moon said in an accepting tone.

The hawk continued to drift. Its feathered wing tips seemed to beckon to her: *Come. This way.*

She turned to watch the bird as it flew beyond the treetops. The movement was too much for the small girl carrying a full basket.

Her weight shifted.

She wobbled.

Her feet lost stability on the loose shale surface. She grabbed for a crevice but lost touch with the rock wall.

She plummeted over the vertical ledge. Colors and shapes whorled into spinning confusion. She flailed her arms into the nothingness.

Thud! She landed in the loose shale at the base of the canyon.

She felt blood drizzle from her temple and tasted it bubbling in her mouth. She could not move her legs but could move her arms some. She could not draw in a single breath of air.

With her eyes, she searched for the hawk.

With her hand, she clasped the rose quartz arrowhead necklace her father had given her on her first menses. She rubbed the pale pink arrowhead with her thumb to feel close to her family and to her clan.

"Grandfather, it's me, Half-Moon," she said, knowing soon, she too would see all the mighty rivers as her spirit was setting itself free.

She knew she would not make the forced walk with the Muscogee to their relocated home in Oklahoma.[1] She released her hold on the necklace as her spirit joined her grandfather's that day.

---

[1] When the Creeks were leaving, one of their chiefs, Eufaula, passed through Tuscaloosa (which was the state's first capitol), and was invited to address the legislature. There are many famous Indian speeches, but it is doubtful if any of them excel in dignity and simple pathos this farewell of the Muscogee chief. His words were translated and taken down at the time: "I come, brothers," he said, "to see the great house of Alabama and the men that make the laws and say farewell in brotherly kindness before I go to the far West, where my people are now going …. I leave the graves of my fathers—but the Indian fires are going out, almost clean gone—and new fires are lighting there for us." (*A History of Alabama for Use in Schools*, Garrott and Pickett, University Publishing, 1900)

CHAPTER 1

The Girl Who Inherited the Rose Quartz Arrowhead

Land is the only thing in the world that amounts to anything for it's the only thing in this world that lasts. Tis the only thing worth working for, worth fighting for, worth dying for.
—MARGARET MITCHELL, GONE WITH THE WIND, 1936

Determined to watch the searchers dig for the remaining body parts, Francie climbed Arrowhead Mountain.

Yesterday all construction on the new highway halted when a piece of road machinery raised its metal claws, unexpectedly claiming two human legs amid the jumble of dirt and rocks it removed while clearing to lay culverts.

The road crew contractors told folks at the Gillivray and Gillery Feed 'n Seed store in Littafuchee that without a doubt the two severed legs did not belong to the same person. One was thin and hairy with a Western boot on the foot. The other leg, dark-skinned and muscular, was shoeless.

Fourteen-year-old Francie Kirwin had felt disappointed something newsworthy had happened in quiet Dixie County on a boring school day.

Enough of the mystery remained unanswered that she had felt drawn to the site on Saturday morning in early June 1985.

Search and recovery crew, working with hand shovels and large sieves, carefully hunted for human remains.

Laurice, Francie's mother, was away at work. Rory, her adopted father, and her Aunt Carmen had forbidden the four first cousins from going to the dig site near their home, Merrifield Farm.

No one had said specifically that she, as the oldest and most responsible, couldn't go alone and watch from Arrowhead's steep cliff directly above where the body parts had been unearthed.

A recreational hiker would have moved in a switchback pattern along the jutting rocks and thorny underbrush instead of straight up the steep incline. Not Francie. The thrill to the athletic girl was to tackle majestic Arrowhead Mountain straight on.

She had made frequent trips to watch the heavy road machinery's progress on the new wide four-lane highway.

Long stretches of it had opened years ago; but like an overlooked stepchild, sparsely populated Dixie County had been put off until last.

This was the last stretch.

Meanwhile, deep rumbling like distant thunder sounded from the excavators and crawlers that dug and pushed relentlessly at the earth's seams of granite, quartz, limestone, and shale.

As a youngster, Francie had been allowed to explore the mountains, foothills, and valley of her family's ranch with her oldest first cousin, Vincent.

Emigrating from Ireland to Georgia then Alabama, five generations of Kirwin children had lived in Dixie County. Their agrarian hamlet of three dozen families, some miles apart, had made scant attempts to modernize for that would bring attention to their all-white enclave in Littafuchee.

Today with the morning sun in her face, Francie dug the toes of her ragged tennis shoes into tight eroded crevices and moved her feet up higher and higher.

She adjusted her orientation for the eye bandage she had to wear over her right eye.

As her thin arms pulled the weight of her body over a lichen-encrusted boulder, her footing slipped and sent rocks plummeting toward Talwa Creek at the base of the mountain.

Like a scared squirrel hanging perilously from a weak tree branch, she dangled from a long kudzu vine. She held firmly onto it and watched loosened rocks roll down.

They bounced off the embankment in rapid succession and landed *plunkety plunk* in the creek below.

Francie wiped perspiration from her face with the front placket of her plaid cotton shirt.

She knew her father would complain again this evening about the road construction muddying the livestock's drinking water. She didn't want to contribute to the water problem and promised herself to be more sure-footed.

Near the peak of the mountain, she worked around to the bald west rim, which overlooked the construction. Here she slid to the middle of the topmost ledge in the mountain's recently blasted stairstep cutaways.

The excavation of Arrowhead Mountain began three years earlier. It was the final extension of the north-south highway and was cussed at by Dixie County farmers like an unwelcomed intruder.

The girl's adopted grandmother, Anne Beatrice Kirwin, a retired Alabama history teacher, had told her proudly of Dixie County's rich local history. She had filled her granddaughter's imagination with lively stories from the Native Americans on to the earliest explorers from Spain, whose interests were in the coastal areas, and fur traders from France.

Granny Bea took her to visit Horseshoe Bend and to Civil War battle sites.

Granny Bea talked about folks from long ago. To many children, they were easily dismissed shadows belonging to their parents and grandparents only. However, Francie could visualize the details of starving, wounded wartime soldiers who wrote home at night by firelight about kissing girlfriends, holding their children, and dreaming of filled bellies from kettles of home cooking. She could feel their homesickness.

Granny Bea recalled odd things that had happened to folks, impossible situations that often sent Francie into giggling fits.

Granny Bea laughed at her own stories but cautioned her granddaughter to speak kindly about others, especially the disadvantaged and eccentrics.

"The poorer someone is, the more pride matters to them," she had whispered to the little girl.

All Granny Bea's stories were wonderfully spun, and Francie had remembered most of them.

She missed her grandmother.

Years ago, Granny Bea was displeased when the official announcement of a new highway was made. It was the same reason local folks were upset. Neither the preservation of the area's scenic beauty nor significant local history seemed to have been taken into consideration.

"Anne Bea has a bee in her bonnet," the county commissioner had warned the director of the State Highway Department.

All efforts to register opposition failed.

Francie shuddered now, remembering how she and Granny Bea would sit on their front porch and listen to dynamite blasts sounding like sky-shattering lightning throughout Littafuchee's valley area.

The windows rattled and the mortar cracked in her family's brick ranch house.

To tear into formidable Arrowhead Mountain, powerful compressors had drilled rods down through many feet of rock. Dozens of dynamite charges went off daily.

After a series of blasts, mighty scrapers and excavators moved in to dig up the rubble while monstrous trucks hauled the heart of Dixie County's most distinguished landmark away, load by load.

The gaping wound was ready for paving. And then yesterday, everything stopped. That attested to the importance of the find.

Sitting cross-legged on the ledge, Francie tried to listen to the muffled voices three hundred feet below.

Tension swirled into the breeze and swept through the gorge:

"… careful, men …."
"… rope this section …."
"… stand back, please …."
"… crime scene. Authorized personnel only."
"Francie."
"… relief crew moving in …."
"Francie?"

Caw-caw-caw screamed a fat crow hovering overhead, jolting Francie into recognition of her aunt's voice calling her name.

"Francie, are you available?" asked the soft, Southern voice to her left side. "I need you to babysit while I go buy some more canning jars."

The girl was startled. She blushed, caught in an act of defiance of Kirwin rules.

"I didn't know you could get up here so fast, Auntie Carmen."

She noticed Auntie wasn't sweating at all.

Carmen said, "I tried stopping you when I saw you cross the creek. But I guess you didn't hear me then either. I have eight gallons of soup mix ready to put up, and I need more quart canning jars with lids. I tried to catch you as you passed," her aunt finished.

She wrapped her long, turquoise-colored skirt around her bare ankles and sat down next to her niece.

"Besides, I must admit, my curiosity's piqued too. What's going on now?"

"Dad's down there," said Francie, pointing him out in the crowd of workers gathered below. "The sheriff's deputy just went over and told him something, but I couldn't hear what."

Carmen rubbed tender longleaf pine needles back and forth in her hands as she watched the scene. She held her hands to Francie's face for her to breathe in the clean, woodsy scent.

Next, she stuck one hand into the pocket of her gathered skirt and retrieved prescription eye drops.

"It's time."

Francie tipped her head backward so Carmen could lift the eye bandage enough to drop in the medicine. She had not been able to see what her eye looked like since the accident except for the small border of bruises on her cheek.

"Auntie, what do you think happened? I mean, nobody in Dixie County's missing."

"Oh, I don't know. Maybe it's the bodies of those two bootleggers they've been hunting for years. The ones who disappeared from one of those coal mining towns. Or maybe some bumbling mortician just had two extra legs and dumped them in the rubble."

"That's not it! Even so, I think it's exciting. I mean I'm sad somebody's dead and all, but just figuring out the whys makes a kid's imagination take off," exclaimed Francie.

Caw-caw-caw, the fat black crow continued to warn the twosome of the dangers below.

Carmen got up. She shook her head no as she glanced at her gold pocket watch necklace.

"Baby-sitting awaits you, my nice niece Frances."

"May we stay for a few more minutes, please? Nothing this exciting has ever happened before."

Carmen waved both arms until she got her brother's attention. He waved back.

"Who's watching the little ones?" Rory shouted to her.

"The TV and Arlo," Carmen shouted back.

He shook his head before turning his attention to the trench in the roadbed that got wider and deeper as the searchers dug.

Francie's attention wandered across the wide span to the other part of Arrowhead Mountain.

There arose the matching notched cutaway that, although it had been part of the same mass for eons, now faced them like an intimidating opponent.

The old Florida Short Route had served as the main thoroughfare for decades. It blended unobtrusively with the natural terrain. The two-lane road twisted dangerously in and out of the tree-lined scenic elevations of Dixie County parallel to railroad tracks, meandering streams, and long white fence lines.

Whenever the Kirwin cousins were in Auntie's van, they pumped their arms at the conductor and shouted to their own driver, "Hurry, race 'em. Beat 'em."

Rolling foothills of the Appalachian Mountain range and fertile fields in the floodplains near rivers and streams made up much of Dixie County. But it was primarily a forest of pines, oaks, hickories, and maples.

Littafuchee had been hidden by the steep mountain range that had proven difficult to traverse by horse-drawn wagon or by foot. The few Anglo-American pioneers who settled in the hamlet lived lives isolated from mainstream society until the early twentieth century when railroad tracks were laid.

For decades thereafter, teenage boys hitched hobo rides south to get off as far away as Columbus, Georgia, or Mobile, Alabama. It was their first exposure to modern cities.

Locally they were known as "elbow boys," clinging by their wits to open boxcars until they could wiggle inside.

As a teenager, Francie's father, Rory Kirwin, had been one of that fun-loving group of teenaged rabble-rousers who typically disregarded the law.

Clustered in Littafuchee were a few lapboard stores, two churches, a gasoline station, and the spacious pristine homesteads.

That was the extent of civilization in a place whose indigenous inhabitants were once known honorably as "those who make straight arrows."

Francie had lived in the little hamlet since she was three years old when her mother married into the Kirwin family. The pleasant view of the farms was all she remembered.

The folks across the new four-lane highway were now like a separate geographic entity.

This separation filled her with loneliness. Her best friend, Kimberlee Gillivray, lived on the other side. She felt stuck on the east side with three younger, bothersome siblings and cousin.

The naïve adolescent longed for everything to be just as it had been during the wonderful years before the terrible road machinery cut a wide divide separating the best friends and the community.

She couldn't figure out why the change had made older folks act so peculiar. They talked about the highway endlessly. Some liked it. Some didn't. Nobody agreed.

Land ownership didn't offer those who'd inherited it a vision of prosperity. Just backbreaking toil. They struggled to make the land profitable enough to hold on to their inheritances.

There were few industries in the impoverished county—a mobile home manufacturer, a poultry-processing plant, and a lumber company.

Locals continued to debate the highway construction's purpose and effect. Most were cynics. Most resented the influx of strange men who came to work on the road construction. For wary farmers and ranchers, there had been a rush to purchase locks for homes and pasture gates.

Francie wished that the crews and machines would work faster, finish, and go away forever so that folks could get back to normal. The tightness in her stomach warned her of what she suspected already: those things will get worse before they get better.

A staccato truck horn sounded. *Shave-and-a-haircut-two-bits.*

She recognized the distinctive sound of her dad's old truck horn. Inside it, one of the investigators sat with Rory. They poured hot coffee from a thermos.

Rory beckoned Francie to come down.

As Francie hurried downhill, her dark brown ponytail flopped against the nape of her neck. Gravity accelerated her descent. She bent deeply at the knees to counterbalance its pull and concentrated on keeping her feet moving rhythmically.

Auntie would be right behind her.

"We're coming, Dad," Francie yelled.

She jumped from the last cutaway to the dirt embankment, then she turned to give her aunt a hand.

She wasn't there.

Shading her good eye against the glare of the sun, Francie spotted Auntie Carmen's turquoise skirt disappearing beyond the pine trees along Talwa Creek.

CHAPTER 2

Rory Kirwin, More Level-Headed than a Fresh Crewcut

I'm in a hurry to get things done, Oh I rush and rush until life's no fun; All I really gotta do is live and die, But I'm in a hurry and don't know why.

—COUNTRY MUSIC GROUP ALABAMA, I'M IN A HURRY

Rory Kirwin was tall and thin yet muscular from years of physical work on the family's small cattle ranch and crop farm where he grew soybeans, cotton, and corn.

He leaned his head out the driver's window as he backed his blue three-quarter-ton truck out of the loose fill dirt and headed south on a roadbed that once paved would be the new highway. He needed to think about the questions the sheriff's investigator had asked him, so he had tuned out the rapid queries his daughter was throwing at him.

Francie enjoyed her one-on-one conversations with her father and that he often said odd stuff to make her laugh. That she was his adopted daughter made little difference to him. He was clearly fond of the teenager. Yet, she worried she would fall out of favor when Vincent, his nephew, returned from the army.

"No whining," Rory had reprimanded the few times she complained about the heat or being hungry when they were out in the fields on the combine at dusk.

Now she wanted to be among the first to know any news he may have gotten from the sheriff's deputy.

"So, Dad, who did it?"

"Did what?"

"Killed the two men."

"It's a fact those legs have danced their last tangos, but who said anybody had been murdered, Ponytail?"

He called her Ponytail because she wore her hair up. Plus, Ponytail had been the name of Rory's 4-H prize-winning heifer in junior high school. She took no offense.

Everybody had nicknames. Her youngest cousin, Jordan, was Shug. Her little brother, Albert, was Bama. Her sister, Beatrice, was Little Bea.

Frances was her given name, but she'd always gone by Francie. She liked Ponytail, too.

In Littafuchee, almost everyone they knew had one or more nicknames with Bubba, Buddy, Elvis, Sonny, and Junior very popular.

"Aw-w, come on Dad. Quit teasing me. What did the deputy say?"

"Not a deputy, an investigator."

"The investigator who was sitting in the truck with you?"

Rory answered, "He said, this is the way a horse eats corn."

He clamped down on her kneecap and squeezed it.

Francie pulled away, giggling.

"Seriously, Dad."

"Seriously? I'm traveling to Ardmore to deliver these steers. And you're going to keep me company."

"Can't."

"Can't?"

"Auntie needs me to stay with Shug and Bama while she goes to Ellisville to buy more jars."

"Bless her britches!" he replied. "I bought her ten dozen quart jars yesterday afternoon. She can't possibly have used them up yet. She just forgot I dropped them by, I reckon. When she goes out on the front porch to get the pressure cookers, she'll find them where I set them down. We'll be back before your Mama gets home."

"I dun-no. I told her I would. I wouldn't want Auntie to get mad at me."

"Ponytail, my sister's never gotten mad at anybody in her life." He paused. His clear blue eyes twinkled mischievously. "It's *Laurice* I wouldn't want to get you into hot water with."

At home his wife, Laurice Fontaine Kirwin, ruled. Her mandates were not to be taken lightly. She gave everyone, even the youngest, responsibilities and expected them to be done regardless. She had to because she worked as a registered nurse and was away from Merrifield Farm most of the time.

Other times, she was sleeping or cranky from lack of sleep.

Francie's job was to watch her five-year-old brother after school and on weekends. She was very protective of him.

Francie wished her mother had any job in the world except that one.

Rory didn't know how they would survive without her income.

Francie leaned out the passenger window and let the air cool her face.

Things looked somewhat distorted with the bandaged eye. She tilted her chin to center her view of the passing landscape. They drove past buckled, weathered wood fencing that marked their shared property line with the Ludekes. They were a kind elderly couple who didn't farm anymore. Next came Pratt Peterson's land. Everyone knew his spread was the best tract of agricultural land in Dixie County because the terrain was level without the usual outcropping of rocks most other farmers had to deal with. Also, he had the biggest indigenous mound in the area which he guarded with a barbed-wire fence within a taller barbed-wire fence. Encircling the thirty-five-foot-tall pyramidal dirt knoll in the middle of an expanse of flat land was such an oddity it drew the attention of travelers on Plank Road as they drove past.

That was exactly what Mr. Pratt did *not* want. He refused to let archeology students from Auburn University or the University of Alabama sponsor digs there.

When Rory was a teenager, he and his elbow buddies drove their motorcycles and ATVs up and down for fun, desecrating the Indian mound according to Mr. Pratt. That's when the double fence went up.

And no one in Littafuchee had been on the mound since.

The cousins had been warned that the disgruntled landowner did not like children trespassing.

Just as some of the other landowners, Mr. Pratt's 240 acres had been cut into two parcels by the highway construction.

His acreage extended over a half mile alongside the newly cut access road that served the three property owners. It turned east on Plank Road with the main part ending down at the river.

The part Francie saw was the dairy business he ran and the milk cows that lolled about grazing on green pasture grass.

He used seasonal workers to harvest his early-season crops of cantaloupes and watermelons. No other farmers could afford to hire a whole work crew of migrants as he did. He grew fields of cotton, which were picked with machinery every September.

Folks' insecurities came out a few times each year. That was always when they saw the county land surveyor's truck parked alongside a county road.

Residential landlines started ringing immediately. The worried voice on the dialing end would ask urgently, "Who died? Who's selling land?"

That's because most of the original settler families who had bought tracts of land ($200 for 160 acres in the mid-1800s) had kept it. These poor yeomen worked the soil with their own hands and built their own structures with lumber from local sawmills.

If necessary, they would deed a parcel of their original homestead to their grown children, if they were getting married and planned to stay in the hamlet to rear their own children. Typically, the parcel would adjoin the homestead so they could share one barn. Young marrieds were given bigger parcels if they wanted to farm the land, not just live on it and work elsewhere. Unless located in the valley, they would need to drill their own wells for water, as plentiful household water for indoor plumbing was an ongoing problem in the rocky areas.

Those who couldn't wait to get away from the agrarian lifestyle, which was the majority following World War II, received in the patriarch's will a few hundred dollars and a few trinkets suitable for city dwellers, such as pocket watches, upright grandfather clocks, a few arrowheads, some old horseshoes, and pocketknives.

The important heirlooms, such as family Bibles (which often served as official records of births and deaths), grandmothers' china cabinets, grandfathers' anvils, vises, grindstones, and prized oak furniture seemed inseparable from the homesteads.

Francie would rather go with her father to the state line than to babysit Shug. Little Bea, her seven-year-old sister, was no trouble at all. And Bama was like a part of her, attached to her side.

"Never any trouble at all" is what Dad often said about Little Bea, his mother's namesake, Beatrice. So that was the way Francie tried very hard to be, too. No problems, good companionship.

Yet, Dad favored Little Bea. He wore a loving, soft expression whenever he was around her. His favorite story to tell was about carrying his curly brown-haired, blue-eyed angel around on a pillow when she was an infant, showing her the farm animals and letting her listen to the birds sing.

No doubt both girls had it easier around Dad than the boys.

From the time Rory and Laurice married, Francie would tag along beside him as he worked and tended the livestock. She had her own tiny galoshes and hard-sole work boots back then because thorny briars threaten year around. Rusty horseshoe nails and forged iron nails used to build the original barn and outbuildings popped out of their holes in changing weather. So, work boots it was most of the time.

In harsh winter weather, a preschool Francie had climbed out of bed at daybreak, eager to go with her father. She'd hold onto his neck. He would put his oversized hunting jacket around them both, zipping it papoose-like to take her up to the small barn while he gave Carmen's milk goats their morning alfalfa.

As she had gotten older, she made herself useful.

Francie often went with him to cut firewood. In the dense forest of pines on the back of their property, she kept vigil over him knowing the dangers of felling trees alone. She poured hot coffee for him and hauled small branches out of the way while he used the power saw.

Francie's revelries were interrupted when the cattle-hauling trailer the truck was pulling began to jackknife.

Rory eased it back into alignment.

"I need a bigger hauler," he commented, adding, "Are you okay, Ponytail?"

"Yes, sir," Francie replied, glancing down the road.

"Dad, I was just wondering, why do we call Mr. Peterson by his first name, Mr. Pratt, and Mr. Ludeke, Mr. Ben?"

"It's a Southern thing for friends and neighbors. Respectful and casual at the same time."

"Mama said it's because there are so few last names here."

"Your mama says that?"

"Yes, sir."

"Mercy. She calls it without sugarcoating."

Rory clutched and shifted into second gear, again for third gear on the straight shift, heavy-duty truck.

"Ponytail, about your last two weeks' allowance, er, would you mind terribly if I paid you next Tuesday?"

Francie studied his face to discern whether he was kidding. She needed her allowance because she was broke.

She'd bought a new pair of athletic shoes during spring vacation when she'd gone shopping with Kimberlee. She'd bought the popular brand shoes with twenty-one dollars of her own money because she wanted something new while Kimberlee's mother was buying her daughter an entire spring wardrobe. Now she was penniless, but she wouldn't whine to Dad.

She watched her father and waited for the ear-to-ear grin that meant he was teasing her.

It was not forthcoming. An explanation of basic bookkeeping did, ending summarily with, "For us, the first of the month payables are staring at me. I'm waiting for Walter Cummings' check to arrive."

A humble, patient man, generous to a fault, he need not apologize to a daughter who saw no faults in him.

Due to the construction, she knew times were tough for his business, Merrifield Farm. Like Arrowhead Mountain, their wholeness had been shattered as preparation for the modern four-lane highway had progressed.

The west parcel had the big barn, outbuildings, the main pasture for the horses and cows, and the dried-up water pond. Some hardwood timber remained, less the pines that he'd sold off.

Due to the highway construction, Talwa Creek tapered to a small stream across the west parcel before picking up Busk Creek on that side of Arrowhead Mountain. There Busk flowed wider and faster. It crossed into the main watershed in the next county.

The east parcel had their house, Carmen's cottage, which was the original log cabin, the springhouse or well house, and the family vegetable garden. Slightly uphill was a fenced pasture for their farm pets, a chicken pen, a rabbit hutch, and Rory's small equipment shed and workshop.

Farther on were acres upon acres of fields where he planted crops to sell and more timberland, less pines that he'd already sold off to the lumber company to make ends meet.

They kept a few chickens for eggs and a few goats to keep the weeds down around the two houses.

Neither parcel of land was large enough to hold the entire herd of beef cattle, so Rory had sold Mr. Walter forty head at one time to fit all the remaining ones on the west side. Now, three weeks had passed, and Mr. Walter's promised check—a final payment—hadn't arrived.

Rory Kirwin felt fulfilled as a farmer but couldn't avoid listening to his inner voice protest being on the losing end all too often. He didn't want to walk in disgrace in the community if he proved unable to dig out of his current financial situation.

Although the highway could bring much-needed change, he reckoned the same blind fates would leave him out of the success stories.

Three other Kirwin patriarchs had worked the same land by growing crops and running a sawmill.[2] They had been hardy men who were without the "book learning" he'd received, graduating from high school and earning a partial scholarship to Auburn. His mother's inheritance had paid for the remaining costs of a bachelor's degree in agricultural science.

Under his tenure as owner of Merrifield Farm, the land had been chopped into two pieces. The money from the state had gone to pay off loans against the expensive modern farm equipment he'd purchased.

Presently he couldn't afford to drill a third well.

True, he felt blessed to be married to a beautiful, loving wife who happened to be a nurse; yet the family had no health insurance.

Like a player in a losing round of poker, he'd let himself be stripped of too many assets while left holding a handful of obligations.

These great financial burdens put Rory into spiritual warfare with himself, questioning his important life decisions. Maybe he should have selected a different major at college. Maybe he should have moved forward with the catfish farm idea when the county extension agent suggested ways to finance it. Maybe he should have taken Mr. Ben's suggestion that they go into the Christmas tree farm business together a few years back.

Maybe Laurice was embarrassed to be married to a farmer who was weathered and used up at age thirty-nine.

---

[2] In 1900, Alabama was a distinctly rural society with more than half its population making a living, such as it was, from a cotton-dominated agricultural economy. By 2000, only 44 percent of Alabamians lived in rural settings and only a small percentage of those rural residents actually worked in agriculture. (www.archives.alabama.gov)

CHAPTER 3

Best Friends Forever

*A teenage girl can survive without a boyfriend, she can survive not being
asked to join the group, she can survive both ridicule and shame; but with a
best friend by her side, she can thrive during her difficult teen years.*

—ANNE BEATRICE, AGE TWENTY-NINE, YEAR 1932

Rory Kirwin waved from his truck window to ladies outside the beauty parlor
parking lot. Francie did too. The southern tradition of waving from passing
vehicles sent unspoken validation and respect to folks, especially to the retired
military veterans from World War II and the Korean War who seemed to pass their
days sitting on porches waiting for cars to pass and folks to wave.

Only two establishments remained standing on the east side of the construction,
Shear Success Beauty Emporium and Remnant Church. Laurice had questioned the
church's use of the Old Testament concept of remnant, implying instead that the
members wanted to keep all others outside their fellowship.

Rory's wife had grown up in Birmingham in the Catholic faith and staunchly
defended it to proselytizing members of any evangelical Protestant church who
criticized Catholicism. For that and the fact that she had not been born in Dixie
County, Rory knew his wife was socially marginalized within the community.

The few stores that gave Littafuchee any appearance of a real place were on the
west side at the junction of McIntosh Road and the old, two-lane highway. These
had anchored the crossroads since the railroad was built at the turn of the century.

Gillivray and Gillery Feed 'n Seed store, a Standard Gas service station with
four pumps (two that worked), a telephone booth that had its own parking lot, a

half-round metal welding shop, and a white cinderblock structure called Harvest Church. These were the tiny Monopoly-like pieces that had survived on that strategic corner.

One railroad track curved through this part of the county and disappeared down a dark green tunnel of pine and mimosa trees and overgrown goldenrod bushes.

None of the living residents remembered Dixie County without the noise of passing trains. On Sundays, preachers prayed and preached right through the sounds. Men welding didn't look up. Farmers in their fields didn't either. Infants and toddlers had the innate ability to sleep through the noisy racket of metal wheels on loose-jointed rails and the shrill whistles of freight trains passing day and night.

For everybody in the valley, train sounds were white noise like automobiles passing or birds singing.

Until completion of the exit ramp and underpass, the two sides of the unincorporated hamlet were reached by locals by driving over the preliminary roadbed.

Rory approached the crossing and stopped the rig. He looked carefully north and south for construction traffic before pulling the trailer onto it.

In the hazy horizon, both he and his daughter could see where the finished part of the new highway bottlenecked into the existing one, and traffic backed up. This was the remaining section where many motorists had lost their lives in dangerous collisions.

Four bull calves in the trailer were to be dropped off in Oneonta. Frightened, they mourned as the rig bumped across the dirt and gravel seam.

"Atmore or Ardmore?" Francie asked.

"Ardmore," came Rory's reply. He took cattle and produce throughout the state, although rarely south where their growing season was longer and the soil better.

Rory pulled up in front of Gillivray and Gillery Feed 'n Seed store, taking up two parallel spaces.

Immediately Francie hopped out of the truck and headed for the store.

"Two Pepsis, ten minutes, and we're on the road, Ponytail," he called out to her.

As Francie stepped inside the old, rickety wooden store, the familiar sweet smells of milled grains, pellets for chickens and catfish, tobacco in all its many forms of use, freshly baked scones, and peanut butter cookies met her.

The earthy smell of boiled peanuts was ever-present, warming in a slow cooker on top of the cold potbelly cast iron stove in the center of the store.

However pleasant these smells were, she did not like the sharp smells of dusting compound, saddle soap, and dill pickles that were ever-present.

With her good eye, she gave a sweeping glance of both sides of the store. She knew Kimberlee would be there because her parents worked in Birmingham. Her childhood friend spent her weekends helping her grandfather in the family-owned business.

Today, Houston Gillivray and Kimberlee were taking inventory when Francie approached them.

"What ya know, hon'?" asked Kimberlee, smiling her perfect smile with gleaming white teeth recently out of braces.

The slight scattering of freckles on her cheeks was in perfect array to Francie.

Kimberlee rehung fishing bobbers and lures on a pegboard frame.

Mr. Houston wrote numbers on a sheet. Without looking up, he asked Francie about her injured eye.

"It's doing fine, Mr. Houston, sir. Thanks for taking me home that day," she replied.

She noticed a shadowy figure through the stockroom arch.

Opalee's here, thought Francie. Her heart began to race. Then the specific smell of Opalee's oily hair and dirty underwear whiffed from her traumatized memory. She gave the young woman, the daughter of the other half of the store, Joe Gilley, a mean glare.

"I'm going to get you back some day," she mouthed to Opalee.

Opalee mouthed back, "I hope you go blind."

"… so Mr. Rory tells me. I'm glad. Hope you get a good report on the twentieth," Mr. Houston's response came, head down, writing.

"Me, too," Francie replied, and then said to Kimberlee, "I'm going to the Tennessee state line with Dad."

"Now?" asked Kimberlee.

"Yeah."

Kimberlee leaned to whisper to her grandfather who was using a wooden crate for a stool.

"Jus a few min-u-ets, Pap. May I p-l-e-a-s-e? Francie's gon-na go so-o-n," she cajoled the old shopkeeper.

"Two Cokes and ten minutes, as usual," he mumbled gruffly with obvious annoyance at their important task being interrupted by a nonpaying customer.

Scampering, the teenagers grabbed one Coke and one Pepsi from the refrigerated case and moved to the front corner of the store. There each grabbed a dried peach scone from a tray, touched the heart of the mannequin holding the tray, and ran lickety-split back to Mr. Houston's half of the old store.

As they drank the sodas, Francie studied Mr. Houston's backside and noted the funny white wiry tufts of hair above each ear and the unusual thickness of his hair. Rotund in physique and sitting on the crate, he looked like a wise owl sitting on a tree limb.

He was regarded by most as the unincorporated hamlet's mayor. Distinguished in comportment and speech, he was Littafuchee's best example of a distinguished southern statesman.

The Gillivray folk all had identical thick auburn brown hair like Kimberlee's.

Kimberlee's mother had explained to Francie that their heritage was Scottish. Their hair color was attributable to genes that were dominant in Mr. Houston's fifteen siblings.

She had continued citing his lineage. The sixteen had come from an even larger generation of Gillivrays with Mr. Houston's grandparents producing twenty-one offspring, minus two that died at birth. The time frame would have covered that of both women's entire reproductive periods.

Years ago, Ms. Vivian, Kimberlee's mother, had used the subject to introduce the topics of menarche and birth control to the two teenagers. Laurice had put her irreverent edge to the discussion by adding that the young women of Dixie County were usually pregnant before many mothers had "the talk."

At the store, bait and fishing supplies sold profitably with deep-water Spearman Lake located a short distance away. As fishermen's last chance to buy bait, along one long wall at the Feed 'n Seed store were four rectangular galvanized minnow vats with filters. Aerated water gurgled through plastic tubes. Francie let her hand direct the minnows' swimming pattern.

She wanted a free gumball from Mr. Joe's side of the store, but the morose man was not around to ask.

Whatever his brother sold on his side of the store (minnows), Mr. Joe Gillery sold something else or a competing brand (fishing worms). He had the identical hair as Mr. Houston but was built rail thin.

"… and he was purdier-r 'n ah poodle sportin' a r-h-i-n-s-t-o-n-e colla'," Kimberlee drawled.

"Who?"

"Gordy! You listnin'?" asked Kimberlee.

Mr. Houston shook his head and replied, "Teenagers! Lawd hep us."

He got up from his perch and disappeared.

Some folks such as Mr. Houston and teachers at school had trouble dealing with Kimberlee's energy; but it fascinated Francie, who was a more serious student. Her understanding of their relationship (cited often by Ms. Vivian) was that she was to keep Kimberlee and her short fuse out of trouble at school.

Kimberlee spoke with the unique local dialect of Littafuchans, who randomly did not enunciate word endings. Ending consonants were softened or dropped. She stretched out words like musical notes on a slide whistle.

Francie liked to get caught up in Kimberlee's passion for things but not her speech.

Kimberlee's unusual poise and confidence compensated for those imperfections. For a strikingly beautiful sixteen-year-old, she caused adults to do double takes. Outsiders stopped to listen to her talk. She gesticulated grandly like her grandfather did. When folks were paying attention to her, she used the same colorful expressions of speech he used, such as "better'n a big bowl of but-t-er-be-ans" and "faster'n a sow swills slo-o-p."

Lately his favorite endearment when referring to the two best friends was "the trouble with kit-t-ns is they grow up to-o-o be ca-a-ts."

If Kimberlee's speech didn't stop strangers in their tracks, her wavy long hair and huge green eyes would.

As she listened to her best friend, Francie continued letting one hand lazily lead the school of fingerlings around the vat while eating her scone with the other.

The overflow water sucked into the plastic filter line, *swoosh, slurp,* like a swig from her soda can.

From outside in his truck, Rory watched Eli, Mr. Houston's golden lab, pull his begging routine on the group of elbow boys sitting out front of the Feed 'n Seed.

The row of odd metal and wooden kitchen chairs lined up in front was a popular gathering spot for them. They were undereducated, underemployed, boyish men of various ages on guard for Mr. Joe. As volunteer watchers, they had been given the job of alerting him of lawbreakers and outsiders, especially Blacks.

Mr. Joe kept a mental hate list of customers who'd passed bad checks or tried to carry concealed weapons into his store.

While keeping watch for Mr. Joe, the elbow boys kept up endless conversations ranging from NASCAR to fishing to hunting to football. The loop repeated throughout the day.

Whomever was sitting out front, Eli came up to him with his slobbery sock monkey and nudged it on his hands.

The dog's simple game proceeded successfully: *I let you look at my favorite toy; you give me a treat.*

The friendly lab's sheepish demeanor and pitiful pleading blinks were effective on folks who fed him scraps of scone, loaf bread, minnows, chewing gum, peanuts, and his favorite "doggie oyster," red worms on saltine crackers.

The dog would not accept offerings of chewing tobacco or plastic wrap with gooey insides due to his delicate digestive system.

Down the row of folks Eli would go until he got full or tired of playing his game. He would shake the sock monkey wildly, walk down the three concrete steps, and lie down at the extreme edge of the old highway where it curves sharply.

Short time is needed for a dog full of junk food to drift off to sleep on a sunny day.

The humane response would be to call Eli back from the high-trafficked crossroads, and some folks did. However, the fun in it for the elbow boys was their own pastime game.

They would bet in boiled peanuts how many drivers would hit their brakes when they rounded the curve to dodge the asleep-not-dead dog lying at the road's edge.

Mr. Houston named all his dogs "Eli," and he'd had a succession of numbered ones. Currently it was the seventh, who'd been around seven years. The elbow boys nicknamed him Lucky.

Watching from midgame, Rory knew that the dog trick these idle men found hilarious was the cause of the intense feud between Mr. Houston and Mr. Joe. It was why Joe Gillery had changed his last name to the misspelled one on his birth certificate (a home birth).

The original "Eli" had belonged to him when they were kids. But teenager Houston, without his brother's permission, had taken the dog to a Labor Day barbecue where a drunk man shot the dog for stealing his pork ribs.

After that, the brothers rarely spoke to each other.

Mr. Joe never owned another pet. Mr. Houston went into adulthood owning a series of dogs and by neglect allowed each one to suffer a tragic end at the crossroads to prove his inhumane position that dogs are replaceable.

As he had yelled at his heartbroken eleven-year-old brother, "When a dog dies, you just get another one."

The relationship remained irretrievably broken as the brothers neared retirement age.

Francie appeared at the front doorway.

"I need ten more minutes, Dad," she said, holding up ten fingers.

Rory held up five for her to see.

"Thanks, Dad. I love you."

Once inside again, the teenagers raced to the back of the store where Mr. Houston's Modern IBM cash register was on the counter on the left side of the doorway to the stockroom and Mr. Joe's antique brass cash register with its button-size keys was on the checkout counter to the right of the doorway to the stockroom. Like children of divorced couples, their paying customers were drawn awkwardly into choosing sides.

Kimberlee shook her can of Coke. It splashed inside. Francie did the same with her Pepsi. "Besties," they exclaimed in unison and swapped cans to finish.

Kimberlee begged Francie to spend the night at the Kirwin home. For all her sixteen years, she had found their family pleasantly unlike her own. They ate meals together, they sang songs together in the car, and they always got colds at the same time because Ms. Laurice and Mr. Rory tucked them into bed and kissed them good night. Even her.

She liked their togetherness or whatever it was called, being a daughter not given much affection.

Francie explained that she could not have her over but promised to do so once the bandage came off her eye.

"Is that when V-i-n-cen' gits bac'?"

"No, but he'll be coming soon."

Kimberlee tugged at her ginger natural waves. "Why hon-e-e- chil', I'd take him ov'r hot but-t-er-ed grits."

Vincent was Francie's nineteen-year-old cousin.

Opalee stepped from a darkened corner of the stockroom where she kept her collection of butterflies and parakeets. To pass the time, Kimberlee's aunt colored in children's coloring books with crayons and looked at teen celebrity magazines.

Her body odor smell hit Francie again as Opalee whispered in her coarsest dialect to her, "I fxckd V-i-n-cen' r-e-e-al good 'fore he lef, Fran-c-e-e."

Francie recoiled momentarily seeing Opalee's scarred face which was a thick mass of brownish scar tissue that covered her left cheek, neck, and what remained of her ear. The ugly childhood scars were hideous for Francie to look at. She had pitied the young woman.

No more.

Opalee was the one who rammed an ivory pickup stick in her eye while the three of them were playing the game on Mr. Joe's checkout counter.

It had happened suddenly. Totally unexpected. And painful beyond measure. Water had gushed from that eye like a deflated water balloon.

Immediately after, Opalee had dropped the antique pick and stood innocently as Mr. Houston and Ms. Dovie applied cold compresses to Francie's eye and then drove her home.

Rory and Carmen had rushed her to the Eye Foundation Hospital in Birmingham where ophthalmologists decided the best course would be to let it heal for two weeks before deciding if surgery would be needed.

"You did this to me on purpose, O-p-a-l-e-e," she sang her retort. "I may never see out of this eye again because of you. Aren't you ever going to say sorry?"

With an empty, evil stare, Opalee looked at Francie. She said in an emotionless monotone, "Dat's a no go. But I'll let ya squ-e-e-ze mah titties. The fellas out front shur lik to."

She pulled her shirt up, exposing her two heavy breasts.

"Shut up! You're a crazy liar about Vincent," Francie exclaimed.

Kimberlee pulled Francie away from the exchange with her kin.

Francie continued in anger, "Close your T-shirt, slut. You're just ugly white trash."

Kimberlee pushed Francie out the door.

As she covered her braless breasts, Opalee shuffled to the store front and closed the door. She returned to her place of obscurity in the darkened corner of the stockroom. Just below the level of self-awareness, she seethed in confused anger directed at all pretty girls, all girls who had best friends, all girls cherished by their fathers.

She would mutilate them all, if given the chance.

CHAPTER 4

Wyatt Hugg, One Decision Away from Stupid

Let me say this: bein' a idiot is no box of chocolates.

—WINSTON GROOM, FORREST GUMP

Dixie County folks had little experience at conflict resolution. Instead, too many folks on both sides of the law had gone missing forever in a county with deep lakes and rivers.

Rory wondered to himself if their stretch of highway construction held that kind of secret.

In the secluded hills and valleys near Littafuchee, there was an unspoken honor code, *nobody wants anybody messing in somebody else's business.* It was frequently expressed as "None of your gol' dern business; and often breeched as "Sum bud-ee know'd for a fact that…."

Especially by outlier Wyatt Hugg.

Wyatt owned the Golden Yokes Egg Farm in a hollow near the east covered bridge between Littafuchee and Spearman Lake.

He identified as part Chickasaw on his mother's side and a descendant of General Robert E. Lee, leader of the Confederate army during the American Civil War, on his father's side.

No one believed him, but that was his own business.

Outside Gillivray and Gillery Feed 'n Seed store, Wyatt leaned against Rory's truck. He had waited for Francie to reenter the store after being granted five more minutes by Rory. He continued sharing his ill feelings toward the elbow boys who refused to let him enter.

Now thirty-eight-years-old, when Wyatt was in tenth grade, he inherited his grandfather's successful commercial egg production business.

Promptly he dropped out of high school and married his second cousin, Edna Mae, who had graduated high school and knew how to type.

His intent was for her to run the Golden Yokes Egg Farm while he took credit for its success.

Edna Mae did a quick assessment and moved all the experienced workers, men and women, into managerial positions.

That was her best decision.

In a few years, she, too, found the business end tedious. She gave them control of the operation. These competent, hard-working employees kept up with modern poultry innovations, eventually moving forward to improve distribution, which allowed Golden Yokes to expand into new markets outside the state.

For two decades, the Huggs had been the most prosperous *local* couple living on Spearman Lake where its miles of lakefront were built out with luxury second homes.

Wyatt hunted or fished year around, leaving his wife ample time to pursue her addiction, shopping.

The Huggs' ignorance and arrogance peaked in 1976 when Edna Mae made a mistake.

After she had spent years filling their six-thousand-square-foot house with every piece of furniture, rugs, framed prints, knickknacks, and decorator pillows she could, she decided to follow her next interest. She aspired to become a tattoo artist.

Wyatt became her canvas. That was a mistake for both of them.

She inked her name permanently inside large hearts on both his upper arms in calligraphy. *Edna* on one. *Mae* on the other.

She inked *Golden Yokes Eggs* in fat block letters on both of his forearms with winsome yellow chicks peeping through cracked eggs (her idea that their advertising agency had rejected early on).

She inked a rare three-legged alligator crawling around and down one calf of his leg and an unfortunate American eagle with tiny wings in flight down the other leg.

The Huggs celebrated their anniversaries with him giving her either another new car or a piece of diamond jewelry. She gave him small tattoos on private parts of his body.

The cars and diamonds were obvious to all. The lower equator tats were rumored as true by ladies at the Sheer Success Beauty Emporium. He became the most unhuggable man in Dixie County.

In 1980 Edna Mae convinced her husband to let her do something special in the ancient art.

"Sure," he'd said agreeably. He liked the needles puncturing his skin. He liked Edna Mae memorizing every inch of his body. He liked the pain she'd inflict because during the recovery period he pretended to be a wounded combat soldier.

However, he did not like the Confederate flag artwork she tried to tattoo like a bandana over his bald head. Edna Mae's perspective could only have been achieved if drunk or on drugs. It was not Camel cigarettes they were puffing the night she traced in the permanent outline.

The outline looked like shaky eyeliner along his forehead and around his ears. From the top of his skull, she had followed his folds of fat for the folds of cloth.

He did not like it.

His wife assured him she could adjust it with green-toned ink.

She did.

The results made it look like he had rings of fungus growing on his scalp. His paranoia crept in. *Is she screwing up on purpose?*

She convinced her husband she could touch up the mistake to where it looked like new growth hair.

He liked that and gave her the go-ahead.

Unfortunately for the amateur tattooist, the added work ended up looking like a Neanderthal's single woolly eyebrow ridge above his real eyebrows and extending ear-to-ear. His scalp got infected and oozed.

After she got out of the hospital with a dislocated shoulder and broken wrist, she decided to take professional lessons.

Later Edna Mae collaborated with the niece of the artist she had met at the funnel cakes food truck at the first annual Alabama June Jam Country Music Festival in Fort Payne in 1982. She taught her inking skills, and Edna Mae helped her set up shop outside Anniston near the army base.

Wyatt began wearing Panama hats pushed down low on his forehead.

Absolutely nobody in Dixie County made comments to him about his Neanderthal brow line because that was his business. Few made eye contact for fear of their own reactions to the debacle. They restrained their smugness, gleeful his stupidity surpassed their own.

Men wore hats and long sleeves for Sundays, weddings, and funerals. Those were the only times Wyatt Hugg fit in.

Earlier, when Wyatt first came up to the truck to lambast the elbow boys, Rory tried to avoid a conversation with him altogether. He had found looking intensely at Wyatt's shoulder mitigated looking at the botched brows. When that failed, he tried whistling.

Wyatt persisted.

Rory stopped whistling and said, "I don't know, Wyatt. One bad action doesn't wipe out another bad one. You may be overreacting. Kind of like bringing a gun to a knife fight, you know."

Within earshot of the row of elbow boys, Wyatt bragged, "Oh, I always carry. It's my right. And I ain't afraid to use it."

He slapped the pistol holster on his belt.

"I think I'll stay out of this," Rory stated firmly. "Picking a fight with them is like stepping in scat. Once you step in it, the smell just won't go away, gets all over everything."

Wyatt paused for a moment. He spat a long stream of snuff onto the asphalt and pressed his hat down tight.

Your rite, Mr. Rory. M-o-r-a level-headed the-e-n a fre-e-s-h cru-cut."

He held the truck door for Francie to get in. He tapped the top of the truck. "Good da-ta-ya."

"Bye, Mr. Wyatt; bye, Kimberlee," Francie called out the truck window.

Slowly Rory pulled out onto the dangerous road as Francie looked at the mannequin wearing Vonnalee's clothes in the window of Mr. Joe's half of the store.

Mr. Joe and Ms. Opal's oldest daughter, Vonnalee, was killed when she was nineteen, precisely where the mannequin stood.

A logging truck lost its load swerving to miss the previous Eli sleeping in the curve of the two-lane. The load of timber came off like gigantic ramrods shooting through the plate glass, beheading their only other child.

While Opalee was overlooked as a scarred-up simpleton, Vonnalee had represented a life of immense potential. She was a willowy beauty queen as gorgeous as Kimberlee but smart. She was the golden child lost to her parents because of a freak accident.

Inconsolable, Ms. Opal lived in perpetual grief ever since. She put a long red acrylic wig on a mannequin and began dressing it in Vonnalee's best dresses—her purple lace eighth-grade graduation dress, her pastel blue shimmering prom gown, and the $5,000 one she had worn as a Miss Alabama contestant.

Ms. Opal started baking pecan scones and chocolate cookies to place on a silver tray that the mannequin held outward in her plastic hands. Folks did approach it for the delicious free treats. In doing so, Ms. Opal expected customers to speak to the mannequin Vonnalee.

The locals did.

So confused was Ms. Opal's mental state that she had the Holiness preacher agree to pray with the mannequin for healing and for the propane gas deliveryman to ask her out on a date.

Francie offered her father the remainder of her pastry. He waved it away.

"Does Mr. Wyatt think the killer's from around here?" she asked.

"Didn't say, Ponytail," he said, taking a swig from Francie's soda, not realizing the best friends drank half and swapped.

He crushed the empty can and threw it onto the floorboard.

"That's strange, don't you think? Not to mention it?" asked Francie.

"Not really. Not considering how small Wyatt's world is."

"It's the same size as mine and yours, isn't it, Dad?"

Rory began whistling. *No need to make Wyatt Hugg her business*, he thought.

CHAPTER 5

Why Would a Kid Ever want to Grow Up?

I wonder if, north of here, they might even run out of stories someday. It may seem silly, but it is cold up there, too cold to mosey, to piddle, to loafer, and summer only lasts a week and a half.

—RICK BRAGG, JOURNALIST, WRITER

Within days, media interest in rural Dixie County waned. Farmers returned to their crops and tending livestock.

Anglers took their bass boats out on the lakes.

Students anticipated the last day of school and the start of summer vacation.

Every chance she could, Francie Kirwin reexamined the known facts about the possibility of bodies buried under the highway.

She stretched her imagination as far as it could go. Bank robbers. Drug warlords. Mad scientists. All were society's evils she knew from television, never in Littafuchee. That is unless the murderer was an ordinary resident of Dixie County with a deep, dark secret hiding somewhere in his past.

As she was stretching her imagination, she and the cousins found adventures to fill their long summer afternoons.

First came sleeping in as a lazy diversion.

Her fifteenth birthday was celebrated with a family trip to Six Flags in Atlanta. Then back to the idleness of hours of daylight to fill.

Their days were nondescript except for the Wednesday afternoon her little brother disappeared.

"Where is Bama?" she said aloud to herself, dropping the book she was reading in the air-conditioned sunroom of their home.

Francie panicked. In the living room the television was tuned to cartoons, yet things were too quiet. She sensed something amiss. Her imagination went to a child snatcher roaming near their farm. A murderer? A madman?

She searched their house under the beds, in closets, beside the gun cabinet. All were her baby brother's favorite places to hide from doing his easy chores.

Convinced he was not *inside* the house, she headed out the kitchen door and quickly up the back walkway, yelling "Bama" until she neared her aunt's cottage.

Auntie's black mixed terrier, Arlo, met her at the woodpile. He yelped and ran in circles around her legs.

"Good boy," Francie said.

She stooped to pat the dog on his soft underbelly. "Where is Bama, Arlo?"

The dog sprawled on the ground nudging her hand with his wet nose. Francie tried to lift his haunches.

"Go find Bama, Arlo," she coaxed. "Go find Albert. He has a ball to throw."

Suddenly as if he understood her directives, the black and white dog jumped up in a frenzy. He scurried under a thick hedge of late-blooming purple Pride of Mobile azaleas and ran to the trunk of the climbing tree in the side yard.

Leaping, he sprang his paws against the trunk of the massive tree and flipped a perfect backward somersault.

He ran around the tree twice, lickety-split, and jumped on it again. Looking up toward the treetop, he waited for Francie. His muscular body quivered with excitement.

All Francie knew was that she'd better have her five-year-old brother, Albert, who was called Bama by the family, found and safe before their mother returned from work.

A barrage of acorns hit her.

"Oh! Ow-w-w!" she screamed. "Stop it, you two."

"Who goes there?" came a little girl's voice.

"Friend or foe?" asked a boy's voice. Then, "State your intent or face certain death by my sword. Gladly will Pirate Angry Hornet and Blackbeard the Fiercest feed you to the sharks below on this very day."

Her first cousin, Jordan Wynn O'Rourke, called Shug at home, was nine-years-old and an intolerable pest who thought up pranks his every waking hour.

Although summer had just begun, Francie's usual patience had run out on him.

Jordan was spoiled and overprotected by his mother who cherished her late in life surprise.

Because he'd remained on the underweight side for his age, his mother plied him daily on concoctions of healthy foods mixed in an electric blender. His first cousin felt sure the foul-smelling green stuff contributed to Shug's pallor and his proneness to mischief.

The whole Kirwin family had been witnesses to his spoiling. The more Carmen tried to protect him, the harder her baby tried to prove himself indestructible. Pestering the girls with spiders and snakes was his go-to maneuver, proof of his intimidating powers in his mind.

Francie climbed part way up the wooden rungs nailed to one side of the tree trunk.

"Is Bama up there?"

"A young man cub is in this dangerous jungle?" asked Shug, stepping into view along his hiding place on a strong outer branch.

Barely an oak leaf rustled under all the small children's weight and movements.

The boy beat his small concave chest with his fists and declared, "I, Tarzan, will help you find the young one before the evil witch doctor does."

Barefoot and sure-footed, he stepped back into the foliage and disappeared.

Francie heard snickering from above.

She straddled the lowest large branch and craned her head upward. The tree's thick summer foliage made human shapes difficult to detect.

With the new highway, a massive southern live oak tree, the General Jackson, came down. Its place of honor had been outside the icehouse in the middle of the split road. Now the Kirwin's towering tree was the largest.

Nailed up decades ago for riders to tie their horses, iron horseshoes were embedded in coarse-textured bark.

During the oak tree's estimated age of three hundred years, their tree's growth had enveloped a chain wrapped around a large horizontal branch that in years past was strong enough to support an engine hoisted up out of a vehicle. Like ugly scar tissue, its main trunk engulfed a gate post and its metal hinges following a time when the house yard had been fenced in to keep out grazing livestock. Heavy branches on all sides grew downward as if gravity would win, then curved up and out into a wide canopy that could shade a hundred people or so.

Dozens of locals had carved professions of love, including ACK hearts ABC (Albert Clyde Kirwin loves Anne Beatrice Cleveland).

Francie knew Granny Bea had loved their climbing tree and had made it the focal point of many outdoor gatherings. She'd said it had welcomed every family member, neighbor, and politician who came up their gravel driveway for a sit-a-spell underneath its deep shade.

Granny Bea spoke to Boy Scout and Girl Scout troops and garden clubs that came to admire her flowers and to learn some local history. Her favorite had been the story of Abraham Kirwin and the tree that talked.

Abe was an itinerant preacher and pelt trader who roamed the lower ridges of central Alabama in the 1830s.

That was a transition time following Alabama becoming a state in 1819 and the Muscogee Creeks being forced to leave their lands in 1831. The Native Americans who refused to leave per treaties still lived in the nearby woods and along the creeks. In 1837, the US government removed the last Native Americans in Alabama to Oklahoma as part of the forced relocation known as the Trail of Tears.

At first there were few settlers along the mountain ridge. There were no hunting shelters to overnight in. Reverend Abraham tried to spot chimney smoke in the valleys to give clues as to which direction to go. None.

Abe came off the mountain ridge randomly when a thick black storm blew in, hiding the dangerous rocky bluffs. He could not see ten feet in front of him. He kept trudging along, wet and slippery, his frame bent into the blowing rain until he collapsed.

Next morning, Abe awoke under the same tree the cousins now called the climbing tree.

During that night, Granny Bea said he thought he'd hit his head against this tree when he passed out. Yet he vividly recalled being in a boat floating across a sea of cloud-white cotton and a vibrating sound telling him to stop.

The talking tree's specific message had been passed down verbatim for five generations, told many times to Vincent and Francie, cousins of the fifth generation.

Go no further, servant of God. This is your new earthly home. Make it prosper.

Granny Bea would smile coyly, pause, and add as an aside that perhaps God's message was a warning to stop because several hundred yards down in a clearing were eighty Red Stick warriors. If he had stumbled into their camp the night before, he would have been slaughtered as an Anglo-American enemy.

To Abe Kirwin, his searching days were over. He squatted on the land until he could sell off his wares and purchase the deed.

As was legally binding, with no other marks found, he carved his initials and last name and *180* into the tree for the number of acres he was claiming. Abraham walked many days to get to Tuscaloosa (the state capital at the time and land grant office) to make claim and to put down his money in full ($200 for 180 acres) paid mostly in American Revolutionary silver coins. While there he filed an intent to claim another 180 acres in the watershed for his brother, Ezekiel.

Settling the area was difficult from the start. Getting over and around the uncivilized area was a dangerous undertaking. The rugged land was a perfect fit for a first-generation Irish immigrant Protestant preacher. He was one of an influx of cotton planters who had courage to homestead under threat of life from the band of Native American holdouts.

He learned they had called the village by the river and the nearby ceremonial field where the warriors rendezvoused Littafuchee. The village had been completely obliterated. Therefore, as happens in the naming of towns and bodies of water, a Native American name was resurrected by European settlers.

Enduring hardships under primitive conditions, he and other Scotch-Irish yeomen and their families became a small part of Alabama's story.

Standing under the talking tree in a wide-brimmed sunhat and gardening gloves, Granny Bea would tell her small audiences that same story, true or not. Exaggerated or not.

Francie had waited long enough. Using her most matter-of-fact voice, she shouted upward into the center of their favorite tree the cousins had renamed the climbing tree.

"Little Bea, if you've got Bama up there, you'd better send him down right now."

Silence.

"You know he's too little to be in our climbing tree. Mama said so."

Silence. Rustling in the branches. A short, fat leg appeared above Francie's head. The bare foot groped in search of a prop.

It disappeared momentarily.

Then two matching legs and dirty feet appeared. They were followed by a roundish body clad in denim shorts and a red-striped T-shirt.

Bama's pudgy body dangled suspended but kicking from the tree branch like a plastic grocery sack that had become permanently entangled in a tree branch.

"Hurry. Hurry up; take him," Francie's sister shouted while lowering him by both hands.

As soon as Francie grabbed him around his waist, Bama was released into her arms. She eased him down to where his feet touched the ground, then she let go.

Immediately the rag-a-muffin took offense. He wrapped his arms around his barrel-shaped chest and, for good measure, stomped one foot.

"I'm telling," he stated stubbornly, which is about the only defense left to the youngest child in a playgroup of older children. For good measure, the preschooler stomped his foot again.

Francie said, "Mama will be on her way home from work soon (a lie). Don't ever run off without telling me where you're going, you hear?"

Bama tuned his back to her and continued pouting.

"Yeah, Bama, listen to your little mommy," chided Shug.

Jordan's short curly blond hair matched Beatrice's curly brown hair. Because the two were the same height and size, in public the two cousins were mistaken for twins.

Francie was convinced Little Bea's brain was missing a few connections. She was too naïve for her seven years of age. While Francie questioned everyone and everything, her sister was the opposite. Unlike Shug's false angelic face, hers fit her appropriately. Wide and trusting. Kind.

Little Bea accepted her position as a middle child with equanimity. She exuded an air of sweet innocence that radiated halo-like above her mass of electrified curls. Because she was sensitive to others' coarseness and moods, especially loud folk, Little Bea's parents shielded her from bad news, funerals, and loud conversations.

Not Francie.

They'd let her experience life's full spectrum of human emotions and taught her to think critically.

"Because you've got fighting French blood in you," she'd been told.

As sisters, Little Bea had an uncanny way of knowing what Francie was thinking or going to say before the words came out.

Francie hoped her little sister didn't know what she'd been thinking about lately. Boys. And sex.

She had spent a lot of time thinking about one whom Kimberlee had told her had come into the Feed 'n Seed store looking for her this summer. His name was Glenn Howton. He was a Kirwin distant cousin from the Spearman Lake area who sometimes sat at her table in the school library.

The last two weeks of school, she'd let him drive her home, a welcome relief from an hour school bus ride.

Glenn was reserved but nice. To Francie, he looked just okay, not sexy, but he was in all AP classes, which was impressive. She was more impressed that he drove a vintage red corvette he and his father had restored and that she got to be seen in it.

He had not given any indication he was interested in her romantically, which was fine with Francie since she could not escape the awkward knowledge that they were related.

CHAPTER 6

Auntie Carmen's Kitchen

Alabama Fruit Cake ingredients: l lb. butter, ¾ lb. sugar, 9 eggs, 1 lb. sifted flour, 2 T baking powder, 2 t mace, 2 t cinnamon, 1 t nutmeg, ½ t cloves, 1-1/2 lbs. watermelon preserves, 1-1/2 lbs. preserved figs, 2 lbs. raisins, 1 lb. chopped pecans, ½ c grape juice

—The Auburn Cookbook, 1962

Carmen O'Rourke's small moss stone cottage consisted of two rectangular rooms—the main room and the kitchen. The long back wall, built into the side of the mountain, kept the cottage cool in the summer and protected from nightmarish tornadoes that swept across hilltops and along valley floors throughout Alabama.

The main room of Carmen's cottage doubled as living room and bedroom. Anachronisms abounded. There was a floral brushed velvet sofa sitting on a room-size rug made of multicolored potholders stitched together; an antique phonograph on top of the television case; a king-size waterbed with a wagon wheel headboard; white French Provincial furniture against knotted pine paneling; and a coal bucket filled with toy dinosaurs and matchbox firetrucks.

Space was crowded yet cozy. The paneled walls, which covered the original logs, were added in the 1920s. They had aged to a mellow reddish brown long ago.

The kitchen was the hub of activity for Carmen's domestic projects.

It held a long worktable in the middle covered with a heavy vinyl tablecloth stapled down. Three highbacked oak chairs with caned seats were at one end of it. Lacquered pine cabinets with flat panel doors lined the walls. Decades and hundreds of gallons of lard frying in cast iron skillets had aged the cabinets to a sticky orange color.

The hand-crafted cabinets held all the bowls and gadgets for Carmen's renowned cooking skills.

Carmen had moved back to Alabama eighteen years prior when her husband died in the Vietnam War.

Her father, Clyde, and Rory closed off one end of the kitchen to make a tiny bedroom for Vincent, her infant son. They added an even smaller half bathroom.

Because of the cottage's elevation up the mountainside and distance from the well, the plumbing didn't work properly. The generator-powered water pump struggled to pump the distance uphill. It made grating, knocking sounds underneath the cottage in the crawl space Carmen use as a root cellar and tornado shelter. She kept the faucet at the kitchen sink open continuously to catch the pencil-size stream of spring water in milk pails for kitchen use. To conserve water, she and Jordan bathed at her brother's house. Jordan urinated off the front porch at night.

Nevertheless, Francie, Beatrice, and Albert were happiest when staying at their aunt's enchanted cottage. Auntie told them that sometimes she heard unicorns and trolls dancing on the roof during the night.

Francie kissed her aunt on the cheek and went directly to the stovetop where she lifted the lid off a pot of fresh green beans. Steam rose to her face. It smelled delicious with onions and bacon drippings. Next to it, chicken frying in a huge skillet splattered grease droplets onto the stovetop like heavy rain drops.

"Anything else for tonight, Auntie?" asked Francie.

Carmen nodded *yes* to Francie as she put a baking sheet of biscuit dough on a shelf in the pantry. Her face was red from the heat that had built up in the kitchen. Her forehead was powdered white with baking flour.

Francie giggled, then said, "Biscuits go in the oven, not the pantry."

"Oops," Carmen replied, removing and sliding the baking sheet onto the middle rack of the heated oven.

Carmen was absentminded about many things, yet she knew how to do everything from crafts and quilts, to gardening and canning, to songwriting and storytelling. Although she worked as hard as anyone around Merrifield Farm, she never wore pants or jeans. She wore either a denim drop-waist dress or a turquoise blue gauze skirt. Except Sundays, she wore a below-the-knee denim apron with eight large pockets in which she kept practical things. She wore her long blonde hair braided into a single rope down her back during the week and coiled it around her head the old style for Sundays.

Pulling out the small bottle of eye drops from an apron pocket, Carmen went to Francie and said, "It's time."

Francie blinked as three drops were dispensed into her injured eye. When the patch was removed, things looked blurry.

"Thanks, Auntie Carmen. I love you."

Carmen took Francie's cheeks in her hands. "Well bless my soul, Frances. You are sweet inside and out."

Then she leaned over and whispered in her niece's ear, "When I get finished, we're going to the railroad cemetery for a picnic. Don't tell."

"Really?! Oh, boy! I won't."

In the main room, the other three cousins were playing Pac-Man on Vincent's arcade. They didn't pay any attention when Francie stepped in.

She liked to look at the pictures on her aunt's dresser that showed the same braided hair and big smile on the wholesome teenager. The free-spirited teen in the picture wore paisley, bell-bottom pants and waved two fingers in the air for *peace*. She still drove the same blue Volkswagen van as then.

Another picture in a gold frame showed a pensive young bride, braided hair wound around the crown of her head with sprigs of delicate white baby's breath blossoms interspersed in the braid. Beside her in that picture stood a fair-haired, handsome young groom in an air force uniform. The airman was Hugh O'Rourke, another of Francie's kith and kin often mentioned by name even though he'd passed away long ago.

"How much soup mix did you put up yesterday?" Francie asked from the main room.

"What? Can't hear you."

"Sh-h-h" sounded the young gamers.

Francie stepped ten steps back into the kitchen and opened the refrigerator. Sealed plastic containers of green beans filled the top shelf. A large bowl of fruit salad sat on the bottom shelf in an orange Tupperware bowl. Beside it was Shug's liquid health food concoction.

"How much soup mix did you can yesterday?"

Francie dipped her finger in the butterdish on the table and dabbed it in the sugar bowl next to it. She licked her finger like a lollipop as she watched her aunt counting to herself.

"Forty. I only put up forty-quart jars. Ten gallons. I need to buy some more early corn and okra from the farmer's market before I can finish the next batch. I know where I can buy some. Those south Alabama produce farmers have been coming into the farmers' market in Ellisville like they're lining up for a FFA parade."

Carmen broke day-old cornbread pone into an aluminum mixing bowl. She shook sage seasoning into it and added chopped celery, butter, and onions.

"I'm working on filling Mr. Joe's order for twelve pint jars next. More if I can, he says. He has folks coming in every day asking for it. I think he's feeding it to Ms. Opal and Opalee 'cause I know he doesn't cook. And I said to him, 'Mr. Joe, you know my garden's too early to pick.'"

Francie opened the oven door. The biscuits were rising and turning light brown on top. She smelled vanilla and saw a golden pound cake baking on the lower shelf.

Strawberry shortcake for dessert, she thought.

She grabbed a hot biscuit off the baking sheet.

Her aunt cooked dinner for both families during the day before her cottage heated up from the sun and from cooking. She packed the food in boxes and toted it down to the main house and set it out on the dining room table.

Francie and Little Bea set and, later, cleared the table. Rory and Laurice washed dishes together while Carmen supervised the boys' baths before getting hers and scrubbing the bathtub.

Carmen washed one load of their clothes each night and took the wet clothes home to hang out on the clothesline the next morning.

Typically, the adults visited a few minutes on the front porch after the serving bowls were clean, dry, and ready to take back to the cottage. Rory or Francie escorted them home with a flashlight.

That was the Kirwins' routine, and it worked with military precision.

"Do you ever get tired of making soup?" asked Francie.

"Nope, my brown-eyed niece. I change it around from week to week. I always put in seven kinds of vegetables so that folks know they're getting a healthy variety. Seven is a holy number, so it's like me blessing them."

Francie took a piece of sliced breakfast ham from a platter to eat with the biscuit she'd snatched from the oven.

"Your choice of *any* seven vegetables, how thrilling," she commented dismissively.

Francie wanted to choose an exciting career. Everybody said she was smart enough to do anything except she didn't know what she wanted to choose for a career. Everything interested her. But she regarded her aunt's talents as constraining and uninteresting.

In school, she was interested in learning about women's fight for the right to vote at the turn of the century. Later came the struggle to get equal pay with the men at work. She had followed Granny Bea's support of the Poarch Creek Indians' efforts for federal recognition. She knew what patriarchy was.

But naively, Francie had met no discrimination that she could point to at school or church. She'd even looked up the word in a dictionary to be sure it was what she thought it was: the recognition and understanding of the difference between one thing and another or the difference between right and wrong.

As a single mother, Carmen had created for herself a home-based business where she made enough money selling canned soup and vegetables, blackberry jam, and seasonal crafts to live financially independent.

Her motto was, "I want to work as long as I live and to live until my work is done."

Francie remembered her grandfather Clyde Kirwin's adage: "service to others." He was a church deacon who had lived his faith seven days a week helping neighbors and visiting the sick and elderly.

He smiled and was happy all the time until his stroke. Poppa had sky blue eyes that twinkled, just like Dad and Little Bea's. He'd sung in a men's gospel quartet for decades until his voice became permanently raspy and uneven.

He was a farmer, a keeper of the soil, plain and hard-working. Poppa's second oft-quoted aphorism was "dirt under my fingernails means food on our table."

Dad used it, too.

Francie asked Auntie, "Have you ever taken Mr. Pratt's migrant workers anything? For free, I mean. Like when you take food to sick folks, just to be of service."

That comment caused Carmen to stop.

"Why, no, Francie. Come to think about it, I haven't. Should though. Why do you ask?"

"I see them digging in the construction Dumpster. Don't they have enough to eat?"

"Don't know. I'll get Laurice to go with me over there soon. I've got two dozen jars that didn't seal. I could take those."

"Why take them something that's already bad?"

"Well bless your britches! They're not bad, honey chil'. Just needing to be eaten soon. My soup mix doesn't sit around anywhere for long," Carmen said assuredly.

She dropped wedges of watermelon into Arlo's dog bowl. He gobbled them up. She studied Francie's face.

"How old are you now? I forget. Twelve? Jesus started asking serious questions of the elders at the temple about that time. Age of accountability or something," Auntie Carmen said, trying to remember.

Francie interrupted, "I'm *fifteen*. One week ago, remember? Six Flags, remember? And I'm not sassing you, Auntie, if that's what you're thinking. Honest."

"That's OK, sweet pea. Questioning is fine. That's how we figure things out."

While Carmen finished her chores in the kitchen, Francie scraped the pots and skillet and washed them for her.

Carmen talked excitedly about Vincent, her oldest son, coming home. She was missing the child she claimed she grew up with as a widowed twenty-year-old military spouse.

Francie agreed with her on point after point.

Yes, Vincent was considerate to call her every week.

Yes, he looked just like his Uncle Rory.

Yes, he would make a good husband for any girl.

Yes, the army was lucky to have him for two more years.

Before Jordan was born, Rory said Carmen doted on Vincent just as she did Shug now. Nevertheless, Rory took pleasure in pointing out that Vincent had turned out to be a fine young man, honorable and trustworthy.

Yes, a fine high school athlete, Francie agreed.

Yes, he was a good soldier, too, although his mother would have preferred the air force.

Francie didn't know who Jordan's father was. Since no one else talked about it, that was one question she wouldn't ask Auntie.

She remembered Granny Bea had said to Carmen, "Lie down with dogs, wake up with fleas." Francie did not know what that meant, but she did know Carmen did not like her mother to say that to her.

"… and all Vincent asked me for when he gets back home is warm blackberry cobbler. That's on Wednesday, er, I think. And that's that," Carmen said, putting the flour sifter, dough board, roller, and can of Crisco in the pantry.

"No, Auntie, that's the next Wednesday."

"Same as. He's coming home. Everything will be great," she said, walking into the main room and clicking off Vincent's Atari game system the little ones were playing fully absorbed in it.

Jordan and Beatrice protested.

Carmen said, "I was thinking about picking some blackberries this afternoon."

Shug Jordan moaned and said he didn't feel well.

"Fresh air will help the collywobbles," replied his mother.

Carmen dropped a book of matches from the mantle into one apron pocket. Shug's Life Savers candy roll went into another.

Then she said, "Y'all could shell some peas or clean some bream for me this afternoon. Or … I was thinking about having a picnic at the railroad cemetery."

Shug and Little Bea clapped their hands and jumped up to get their shoes from the front porch. Francie buckled Bama's sandals on him. She stepped out of her flip-flops and into her work shoes for walking the rough terrain.

Carmen stepped back into the kitchen, then reappeared with a heavy flour sack bulging with picnic goodies. She slung it over her shoulder and headed out the front door. She held out a tomato wedge to get the dog to follow her.

"Come on, Arlo."

He jumped off the waterbed, grabbed it from her hand, and gulped it down in one piece. He burped loud and long for a small dog.

Everyone laughed.

Arlo trotted importantly alongside his mistress.

Francie, Little Bea, and Bama got in line behind them, following their aunt into the woods.

Shug grabbed his air rifle off the porch and joined them.

"A picnic in the cemetery! Yea!" they echoed.

CHAPTER 7

Strangers in a Strange Land

The choice was whether to be sad and foolish or sad and reasonable.

—VICKI COVINGTON, WRITER

While on her daily rounds as a home health-care nurse, Laurice crisscrossed three counties.

Often her thoughts returned to Merrifield Farm and to her family there. She missed them.

Her sister-in-law, Carmen, was indispensable. She made it possible for her to return to work after having Beatrice and again two years later, Albert.

She loved her husband, Rory. She did at first sight that cool autumn night at Vulcan Park on Birmingham's Red Mountain. They were each there with other dates and passed once in the winding stairwell that went up 159 steps to the statue's observation tower. The second time was at a park bench along the wooded trail below the statue of the god of the forge that overlooked the twinkling lights of the Steel City's downtown area in Jones Valley below.

There under the bare tree's sway and lit by waves of magical moonlight, the two couples began chatting about football—the Auburn-Alabama game that was to be played the next day. She wore Alabama colors. He wore blue.

He had said his name was Rory. Unusual, not Roy, but she liked the sound of it. She tuned out the other two young people completely and began flirting with the handsome, mesmerizingly blue-eyed country boy in tight blue jeans who came across as intelligent and witty.

It had taken a mere month of dating for Laurice to realize the former city girl was going to live out her life in the middle of rural Alabama amid cows, pastures, washboard dirt roads, and occasional outhouses.

As she was introduced to family, neighbors, and church family, Laurice found them alarmingly disarming. Quaint. Genuine. Humble.

They lived low income lives without frills. Their activities revolved around church and family. Their conversations were simple declarative sentences about weather, crops, and children.

Laurice was puzzled that they didn't ask her personal questions. Not at all. They could see she looked different with creamy skin, brown eyes, and black hair. Did they realize she was of French descent, not Italian? That she was widowed within one year of her first marriage due to the war?

The gentle country folk of Dixie County she'd met enjoyed taking her on tours of their modest homes, giving details about their collections of teacups and figurines. They showed her their handmade crafts and ended with walking tours of their flowers outside. As a rite of departure, each family insisted on sending her on her way with something from their home and hands. She'd been given market baskets of yellow crookneck squash and bundled turnip greens, iris bulbs to plant in the fall, and hydrangeas rooted in coffee cans to plant in the springtime. The women continued the tradition of gifting intricately crocheted doilies and Christmas ornaments made from nature.

There were so many positives to be considered that she decided to fall in love again, this time with the farm families around Littafuchee.

She was determined to fit in even though in 1972, the world outside the hamlet was going to hell on an express elevator down. George Wallace was shot. Industrial smog and water pollution were news items. National news was about the Watergate Scandal, the ongoing Vietnam War, the massacre of Israeli athletes at the Summer Olympics, the Apollo 17 spaceflight, and women and gay rights.

None of the locals registered interest in current news topics.

In many ways for Laurice, the hamlet was a blessed escape from reality. A simple existence.

Rory's family accepted her toddler, Francie, from the start.

At the end of month two with bridal stardust in her eyes, Laurice Fontaine decided to stay in Littafuchee with her country boy.

She spent hours learning from her new mother-in-law, Anne Bea. She taught her how to shuck and cut corn and fry meats.

Mama Bea had said to her, "Farmers are like teenagers, always hungry. Throw something in a pot of water to boil. Then fry chicken or pork chops or steak. Our men will eat everything on their plates. Put butter or fatback in with whatever you're cooking, and they'll eat everything in the pot. Just be sure to cook plenty of it."

New to Laurice were meal staples. Cornbread and sweet iced tea could be served at all three meals, as could sliced tomatoes and cucumber pickles. Tossed salads were foreign food to the Kerwins. Cole slaw was served on the dinner plate with the other food, touching. Buttered biscuits with sorghum syrup or apple butter made a satisfying "poor man's dessert."

Laurice became Mama Bea's project. She called her daughter. She was determined to equip Laurice with all she needed to know about her son from his birth onward. She listened to every story and laughed at his misadventures. She learned where to put the Tupperware and Corning Ware. She knew where Clyde kept a fifth of whiskey (in the shoeshine box). And that Laurice was never to walk into the tool shed toward the end of a workday when Clyde and Rory *relaxed*, as she called it.

"I've never seen a church deacon who drinks," Mama Bea declared, then winked. "And I don't intend to see one at my age."

Her mother-in-law's love story was similar in many ways to Laurice's, except two generations apart.

Mama Bea had come from a prosperous family from Montgomery. She was much older when she married. She had been an independent woman teaching school in Ensley and living in a women's boarding house near Birmingham-Southern College. Admittedly, she had wondered if God would find the right man for her before she hit the spinsterhood marker, thirty years old. All seven of her siblings had graduated from college and all had careers in education or engineering. And families. She was the last to marry.

After her marriage to Clyde, she taught history and physical education at the middle school in Ellisville. Just as southern men live and breathe sports, she breathed Alabama history. Like a walking textbook, she attached a fact about Alabama's early history to each conversation. For that, Laurice found Mama Bea the most interesting person in Dixie County.

There had been like-minded teachers Anne Beatrice Kirwin came to know who had married farmers from Dixie County also. These sophisticated, motivated educators converged into the subsistent area through marriage during the early

1920s and on into the Great Depression. These determined women coaxed the hill folk into better existence, at least concerning progress that made their lives easier.

The female schoolteachers campaigned to have electricity run into homes on unmarked roads, then advocated for electric washing machines to be sold at the Feed 'n Seed. Anne Bea convinced Houston and Joe's parents to accept small payments from the locals each month with her as guarantor.

In the early decades, the women talked to groups about the risks with home births. Later they encouraged birth control in the same ladies' groups. They invited nutritionists to come speak to church groups and ladies' quilting clubs.

At school in the early decades, these teachers knew they were trying to teach academic subjects to some students who lived in homes with dirt floors, who slept three or four to a bed, and who had never traveled to a single major city in Alabama. Of these, many had never seen a driver's license, a newspaper, or a set of encyclopedias.

Mama Bea told Laurice that the progressive-thinking, compassionate educators always respected the illiterate person's dignity.

"If you can't walk in a poor man's shoes to understand him, walk beside him to help him," she admonished her new daughter-in-law.

The group of teachers began a volunteer project soon after Anne Bea arrived to teach basic literacy to interested adults. By offering in-depth remediation in the homes of those students from illiterate households, they had hoped all the family members would benefit from listening to the simple alphabet, reciting arithmetic drills, and hearing current events read aloud from newspapers. She recalled one student no longer shamed because he had to print out his parents' names beside their "mark" on his report cards.

A few homes were so remote that a couple of daring teachers rode donkeys down long impassible trails to reach the primitive homesteads. After dark by lantern light, someone would walk each back to the main road.

This small group of volunteer tutors equipped deep wood folk sufficiently to where the yeomen farmers were able to sign papers, contracts, and loans—an affirming step toward doing business with the outside world.

Zero, the teachers' pay for this effort, was intrinsically satisfying to them for years.

Invaluable, the parents' reward was elevated status. They were no longer illiterate.

In her cycle of repeated stories from the long ago past, Anne Bea often told of playing on the first Auburn women's basketball team.

Another was when as a physical education teacher, she formed a hiking club. About a dozen students signed up although they had no idea what a hiking club did.

On their first venture, which was to the top of Arrowhead Mountain, they followed their teacher who was cutting a trail with a sling blade though the underbrush.

When they got to the top, the students asked their sponsor, "What do we do now, Mrs. Kirwin?"

Looking out at the dozen shades of green vistas rippling across to the far horizon, she suggested, "Take joy in reaching the top. You've met a physical challenge successfully. Now sit. Here's your reward. Look at that! How big the world is!"

"Tune in to nature and its beauty. Truth and beauty grow the soul," she concluded.

Used at home as free farm laborers, the middle school students remained confounded. Endless chores and bone weariness had not facilitated philosophical rumination. Only one awakened soul would write poetry in high school. Few graduated. Fewer attended college. Most remained on the family farms.

Anne Bea's ability to instill confidence in folks was the unique feature of her personality. In her classroom, she examined issues critically, intelligently, and encouraged her students to safely express their own informed opinions. Twelve- to fourteen-year-old students took notice that they could use informed opinions outside the classrooms, too.

Anne Bea advocated to parents for her students to get seven to eight hours of sleep each night. She allowed them quick naps on their desktops during school. She brought candy on Fridays. Birthdays were celebrated in homeroom. The poorest students in her classes took delight in her attention to them.

Conditions improved when former students' children became her students. These were bright children reared by literate parents who lived in homes with standard plumbing and electricity or in new contemporary low ranch style brick homes. Still, Ellisville and Spearman Lake students set the standard for test scores.

Anne Bea's heart and focus was on the middle school students of Littafuchee. She wanted them to be prepared for high school success. Each new school year she identified a few exceptionally bright students from Littafuchee whom she challenged academically and took symbolically under her wings to begin to enrich their lives on her own time and at her own expense. She was always pleased at these students' progress.

The details of early poverty that Mama Bea shared with Laurice overwhelmed her, like hearing a never-ending horror story. What Laurice herself experienced in poor patient homes five decades later seemed minimal comparatively.

Mama Bea's recollections were intended to show Laurice how far Dixie County had come in fifty years. Even after retirement, she and Clyde kept involved with a group of civic-minded movers and shakers in Dixie County. She was clearly proud of the progress made since the late 1920s.

"I will until I can't" was Mama Bea's catchphrase.

Her influence and determination ended three years after her cancer diagnosis.

Laurice grew up in Birmingham during the racial protest years. She had witnessed and been caught in the middle of the conflict that seemed to have no permanent resolution. Change was resisted. Conflicts reignited.

She knew her children, Frances, Beatrice, and Albert, lived in an all-white enclave and were unaware of what awaited them. Their lives were sheltered and idyllic. Why would she want her kids to grow up knowing the world's turmoil?

She felt blessed to be the mother of three innocent children and comfortable with the Kirwin's bucolic lifestyle. Like the Native American Creeks and Cherokees who walked on their land first, hers were children of the forests, close to the earth and nature.

Right? And wrong.

As a commuter and weekend parent, Laurice had failed to recognize the secrets, hatred, and violence these same open spaces held.

CHAPTER 8

A Mere Decimal Point on the Road

I think a place can be as much a character in a novel as the people.

—FANNIE FLAGG

The traffic exiting Birmingham was congested, almost at a standstill. Laurice Kirwin was tired after traveling one hundred miles over three counties making her rounds on six patients recently discharged from the hospital.

As vehicles inched along, she reviewed in her mind what she had learned from her eleven years traveling rural Alabama.

First, country folks had a covetous appreciation of the land they lived on, especially if their direct descendants had lived on it. They liked the open spaces and the privacy. Country folks could do anything they wanted on their land if they felt their ancestors would bless their efforts and continue to watch over them in spirit.

Farmers begot farmers, horse trainers begot horse trainers, preachers begot preachers, and day laborers begot laborers.

She saw in coal mining towns the same generational occupations.

She visited patients who were steel workers of third and fourth generation iron and steel workers. Their literate women were locked into supportive, domestic roles with large families and held back by scarcity of employment opportunities in small towns.

Part of Laurice's job was to listen to her patients. Ancestor worship was a quaint characteristic of them all, a frequent topic of low- and middle-class culture, just as prominent legacies were important to upper-class people she had met.

Country folks' powerful memories of family from past generations followed them daily, like friendly spirits walking among them, whispering to them: *Time to repair the barn. Time to mend fences in the south pasture. Time to pick the pole beans.*

And that's what they'd do, health and age permitting.

Second, in all her home visits, she had seen family genetics replicated in multiple versions from elderly folks to newborns. Theirs was unmistakable kinship bound together by some unmet ancestor from generations prior. They had similar health problems and lived similar life spans, all things equal except smoking, dangerous occupations, and nutrition.

In her own county, the interconnectedness of the various families was a bewildering spider web to her. She had stopped trying to figure it out and just accepted that every person living in Dixie County was either directly or distantly related with common last names.

Some days, she felt a stranger in a strange land. The clans. Their churches. Their lack of curiosity about the world. Their ingrained responses to the powerful demands of the earth upon their labors with a seasonal force she'd observed but didn't feel.

What she'd experienced in eleven years often felt to her like a fierce wind slamming her into unexpected directions. She was the stranger forced to bend to the local traditions and customs. They did not want to hear her life experiences.

By the time traffic lightened, she'd concluded that her remaining life would be a journey toward acceptance by the existing closed subculture. Maybe she would make it. Perhaps more social invitations would come. Sometimes she felt lost and alone, a sorority sister without a soul sister in sight.

Her sexual attraction to Rory remained so strong she would walk through fire to support him and the land he treasured more than gold. The land he walked was family land. His goal was to keep it intact to pass down to his son and nephews without dividing it.

The orange traffic barrels narrowed the cars' spacing as she got to the exit. Quickly, tractor-trailer rigs slowed, as did oil tanker transports and recreational vehicles the length of mobile homes.

Every vehicle had to inch through the intended funnel and onto the old highway to proceed for thirteen miles through a treacherous winding two-lane.

All day she had remembered it was the seventeenth.

The dutiful daughter followed her own version of the South's death culture. She had her ritual to follow. It brought her order and peace of mind even though it took her back monthly to the spot in the narrow highway where both her parents had been killed eight years prior.

She pulled her car off at the shady pull-off across from Busk Creek and what remained of a stacked rock wall from the Civilian Conservation Core project built in the 1930s during the Great Depression. She reversed her car to face the scene marked by small white wooden crosses.

She shivered. The shady ravine was cooler than the ninety-degree weather elsewhere.

She grabbed for the shawl in the backseat that her mother had knit for her years ago. Laurice let a small smile creep into the corners of her mouth. Her fingers rubbed the flame-stitch pattern of yellow and orange yarn. Her eyes rested comfortably upon each irregularity in the pattern—a dropped stitch, a small hole, a Grapico stain.

In the quiet air-conditioned capsule that was her car, she let an even bigger smile grow followed by a heaving, mournful sigh. Remembering and crying were integral to her ritual.

And self-medicating.

She took a swig of Jack Daniel's bourbon whiskey, her father's favorite brand, between lines of vehicles whizzing past.

Unlike the pattern and imperfections in the shawl, the vehicles were nondescript to her. Blue sedans were indistinguishable from green ones, new trucks from old trucks, oil tankers from timber-hauling rigs.

Her mental state cycled between confusion and outright anger that her own parents' car did not make it safely around the narrowest of many hairpin bends in the road. Head-on her father had encountered a coal truck whose own driver had overcorrected his shifting load.

In an instant, Laurice had become a motherless daughter. Within forty-eight hours, an orphan.

What she sought from the whiskey was numbness. She toasted the vehicles traveling safely today with a final swig and then tucked the flask inside her purse.

She heard a *crunch* sound. The gravel pull-off.

A silver Lincoln Continental squeezed into the small space beside her car.

Laurice watched curiously.

Dovie Gillivray, Kimberlee's grandmother, opened her car door, quickly exited it, and slammed the door shut. She walked up to Laurice's window.

"May I?" she motioned to the passenger seat.

Trim with stylish hair teased on top and pulled asymmetrically to one side of her face, Dovie waited for Laurice to move her brown baggy purse and nurse's cap from the passenger seat to the backseat with a quick toss.

Dovie sat down. Her small blue clutch placed in her lap, she shifted to her left hip and faced Laurice.

"How's Frances' eye?"

"It seems to be healing. She's got an appointment Monday in Birmingham. The Eye Foundation. They'll let us know how much vision was lost."

"Good, dear. That's good."

The two women sat in silence for a few awkward moments. Laurice felt sheepish before this popular schoolteacher. Her guard was full on about her whiskey breath. She wrapped the shawl protectively around herself.

Dovie said, "Frances was an excellent student. I enjoyed having her in my eighth-grade homeroom year before last."

"Thank you."

"She will make it out of here. Most don't."

"I know," Laurice said affirmatively.

"What's her sister's name?"

"Beatrice. We call her Little Bea."

"That's right. I forgot. After Ms. Anne Beatrice."

"Yes."

"Well, if she's anything near the go-getter her grandmother was, she'll do wonderful things in life too."

Laurice nodded *no*. "But she's not. Not like her Granny Bea or Francie. Like me."

"I see."

The traffic on the two-lane continued to pass by in random lines of three or four, always led by a slow driver.

"I see," Ms. Dovie repeated. "I specialize in sensitive students."

"How's that?"

"In my forty years of teaching, I've noticed shy, er, sensitive students tend to get overwhelmed easily. With school overcrowding, we've had up to forty-five students in a homeroom class. *Tsk. Tsk.* So chaotic," Ms. Dovie said reflectively. "Once I sense a student's getting vexed, I'll give him or her a simple assignment like sorting supplies in the coat closet."

The educator continued, "I had a shy, smart girl many years ago who'd become physically sick smelling the odors in there like bologna sandwiches and mildewed rainwear. I moved her with another good student out into the hall, set up a desk, and let them grade math and spelling papers for me. They loved it! This girl thrived. I let them make up discussion topics from the upcoming *Weekly Reader*."

Laurice smiled a genuine smile. She knew Ms. Dovie's reputation at the middle school as a miracle worker with difficult students.

"Was it Carmen?" Laurice asked coyly.

"Yes."

"She said you got it that she thought differently than most."

"A creative spirit following her own path!"

"That's not Francie!" declared Laurice. "She's not reticent at all."

"No, ma'am, she's not," agreed Dovie. "Frances likes leading group projects and organizing games. She's confident. Curious. I predict she'll leave the high school with an academic scholarship."

"Well, as y'all say around here, 'Praise the Lawd!'"

After their amusement settled, there was more awkward silence.

Dovie spoke heartfelt, "I remember what happened here."

"You do?"

"Horrible. A most tragic way to lose your parents, Ms. Laurice."

"The day I became an orphan," Laurice stated flatly, but for the first time aloud to anyone.

Tears began to fill her eyes.

"Lawd-a-mercy! And bless your heart! You had and you have a big, busy family to be very proud of. No orphan you, Laurice Kirwin."

"Proud? Ms. Dovie, I have feral kids running wild in the woods being babysat by a hippie and a dog!"

Dovie placed a hand on her shoulder softly. Laurice forced tears back and turned her thoughts outward.

"Honestly, I hate to go home after work. All their yammering at each other … all … the … time. I was an only child. My house was quiet. Things organized."

Dovie started to speak, but Laurice continued.

"I guess I just need time to refresh from seeing elderly patients called Bubba and

Junior or a Lee middle name. I travel county roads where Confederate flags wave at me from trucks driven by young men born four major wars *after* the Civil War. It wears on me.

"And at this damned decimal point along this highway, I just need to acknowledge that everything changed for me *right here*," she said with emphasis.

Accustomed to students' outbursts, Dovie put her hand on Laurice's and waited. Silence was appropriate.

When Laurice regained her composure, Dovie said softly, "You need to find you a quiet coat closet, safer than the one we're at right here. Promise me you will, dearie."

"Yes, ma'am, I will," Laurice lied.

But she had been heard. Someone in Littafuchee cared. Someone had given recognition that a major life-changing event had happened to her, a woman still grieving loss and overwhelmed by the noise of family life.

After Dovie departed, Laurice kissed the cross hanging from her rearview mirror.

She made the sign of the cross across her front:

Hail Mary, full of grace, the Lord is with you. Blessed are you among women and blessed is the Fruit of your womb, Jesus.

CHAPTER 9

Thrills and Chills on Cemetery Hill

*The nice thing about ghost stories is
that you don't have to believe in ghosts
to enjoy hearing a good ghost story.*

—Kathryn Tucker Windham

The youngest cousins plus Carmen Kirwin O'Rourke hiked northeast alongside Talwa Creek.

They followed an old lumber road through second- and third-growth forest of pine, maple, and sweet gum trees. Auntie Carmen cast out sprinkles of clover seed to stop soil erosion where loggers' equipment had ravaged the land like a tornado's destructive path. Not far off the path, a few nineteenth century log structures and a moonshine still layout near a small stream were barely visible from decades of decay and voracious kudzu vines that covered and pulled shallow objects into the soil. Regularly, Rory brought the goats to eat and keep the invasive kudzu in check along the lumber road.

Short legs walked very slowly. Auntie encouraged them along singing her choppy, made-up song, "Go Outside, Play in the Dirt, Don't Come Home 'Til Dark."

Beatrice and Albert dawdled to pick dandelions, chase butterflies, and collect interesting rocks.

Jordan chased Francie into the woods twice with a dead crow carcass he'd found, although he claimed he'd shot it with his air rifle. In retribution, Francie threw baseball size rocks at him.

I will steal his gun as soon as he puts it down, she thought.

She followed the group toward the railroad cemetery from a safe distance along a deer trail to keep away from her pesty cousin.

As the joy of being in nature filled her, Carmen began next to sing aloud an inspiring call to worship that expressed her spiritual connection to God and nature.

"For the beauty of the earth
For the glory of the skies
For the love which from our birth
Over and around us lies.
Lord of all to thee we raise
This our song of grateful praise."[3]

Little Bea's bouncing curls collected an assortment of twigs, cockleburs, and webs as they walked.

She looked up and said innocently, "The trees like us to be here, y'all. Hear that sound they're making?"

She curtsied in one direction, then another. "How do you do? Green's my favorite color, did you know that, trees?"

Auntie Carmen took Little Bea's hands, and they did ring-around-the-rosy. "You are my spirit child, honey Bea. Let's dance for the trees."

Deep in nature's cathedral of tall pines and majestic oaks, underneath a glorious blue dome of infinite height, and with the rushing stream whispering *peace to all*, the hippie and her charges met God. They danced and twirled before Him. They laughed and vocalized, "la-la-la," for Him. They breathed in His breath and received His music to themselves. And when they were satisfied that He was everywhere, they stopped to rest.

Resting on their backs staring up at their outdoor church, they connected to each other away from the distractions required to fit into mankind's world. They heard a euphony from nature's choir – cicadas, bugs, frogs, birds, leaves, wind.

In time one of the cousins said, "I hear a squirrel climbing a treetop. I see the nest."

"I hear a woodpecker knocking in the distance. I see a red cardinal watching us."

"I feel soft winter's leaves underneath my legs."

"I'm hungry," said Bama.

Auntie passed out small June apples to each child.

---

[3] Words by Folliott S. Pierpoint.

"I see an apple stem."

"I hear a loud crunching."

"And a lot of smacking."

"I taste a sweetness that's not like white sugar."

"I've got juice running down my chin," said Bama.

"I see Mom's handkerchief."

"I hear Bama throw his apple core into the woods."

"I feel Auntie's handkerchief on my chin," said Bama. "Thanks, Auntie Carmen."

"Bless your little heart, young'un."

They sat up to finish their apples, leaving a little good fruit for the forest's smallest critters. They tossed the cores underneath bushes for them to find.

Arlo did not share his apple, eating the seeds and stem too.

Auntie pulled Bama up by one arm. Then Little Bea.

Shug reached to pick up his air rifle as he stood up. Francie grabbed it and took off running toward Cemetery Hill with him in pursuit.

Fifteen minutes later, the journey ended near the railroad tracks at the site of a neglected cemetery where four dozen or so grave sites were sunken and weed-covered.

The cemetery was up a ridge directly behind an old train depot, long abandoned. The depot's basic rectangular shape was wrapped heavily in twisting kudzu vines that grew toward the morning sun and reshaped the building into a dangerous leaning structure.

Erected in the 1910s, its services as a mail and supply drop had not been used since the 1960s.

A few of the graves in the place called Cemetery Hill by locals had small white marble headstones. A few more, larger and more recent ones, were gray granite. The others, marked with crude sandstone slabs, indicated slaves buried there.

The markers seemed to be laid out haphazardly; but upon closer inspection, a visitor could discern that shared family names created a scattered group layout of landowners and slaves with the same last name together but apart.

Francie tried to read the weathered inscriptions: 1859 John Zavier, Sweet Infant Son of Ennis and Zola; 1875–1902 Katherine Kalen, A Goodly Wife and Christian Woman; 1918 Coot Kirwin, WWI.

Today chipmunks played chase over and around the headstones. The humans did not stop their fun.

Carmen took her son's air rifle away from Francie.

On some headstones the inscription, CSA, meant a man or boy who had served in the Confederate States of America during the Civil War. Auntie Carmen explained to the children that there may not be an actual body buried in plots because many casualties had been buried on the battlefields where they fell, so families placed memorial markers to commemorate their fallen soldiers.

Carmen brought her young charges to the cemetery twice each year because, she'd told them, she was fond of spotting deer and other wildlife along the way and because the spirits of the deceased awaited visitors.

The past October, the Kirwin family had camped out overnight just below the cemetery. They had walked the railroad tracks at night by moonlight and flashlights. It was scary but fun for the cousins.

As then, Carmen had come to Cemetery Hill today prepared with spooky yarns mixed with a little history. The cousins would have preferred it no other way.

Jordan prodded his mother. "Is it true that dead men's hair and beards keep growing?"

Carmen squinted one eye at him and grimaced, giving his question pseudo serious thought.

She set the flour sack down and took out the picnic items. On the ground in the shade of an oak tree, she spread the sack for a tablecloth. Then, meticulously she arranged a package of wieners, crackers, cheese, chips, and Kool-Aid.

The young cousins watched her with anticipation.

Slowly Carmen's demeanor began to change. Her facial muscles tightened and her chin poked out as her neck elongated. With alert movements, she looked in all directions as if she'd heard something approaching. When she spoke in rhyme, her voice was witchlike and gruff.

"Cold bodies, deadly heat, tell me quick, how do you want yours to eat?"

Huddled together and puzzled, the cousins looked around at each other.

"Your hot dog," coaxed Francie.

"R …. R … roasted," whispered Little Bea first.

The others the same.

"Gather some twigs before ghosties call, make a fire, but keep it small," she ordered in her menacing voice.

Francie jumped up, "Hurry!" she ordered the others. "Before they get us!"

"W … w … who?" asked Bama, near tears and grabbing onto his big sister's hand.

Shug dropped a handful of twigs in a heap in a clearing beyond the tree's canopy where they'd built debris fires in the past.

Then he said to Bama and Little Bea convincingly, "Them be—ghosts … or goblins … or witches … or something."

His mother nodded. "It is evil I sense moving through today. Yep, they can move *right through* a person and mess them up for life. There are more ghosts than angels here. More snakes than Moses can shake a stick at. So hurry, y'all. You ought to make quick work of it before they get us."

"Who?"

"What?" the cousins queried as they ran around the cemetery gathering fallen tree branches.

While they were busy, Carmen arranged their offerings in a stack on the gray ashes of an earlier fire.

Reaching into an apron pocket, she pulled out the book of matches and a twisted length of lint. She lit the dried leaves in the center of the brush fire.

Beatrice's eyes widened. "*Through?* Oughtn't they be more interested in going through *big* like Francie than *little* like me?"

"Yep, and maybe," replied Auntie because not answering conclusively was her way of not libeling herself.

Goose bumps raced up Francie's arms. The responsible big sister gathered Little Bea and Bama close to her, partly for her own protection.

Bama reached up for her to hold him. She hoisted him onto her hip and wrapped her other arm around her little sister.

The storyteller bent over the fire as it began to flame and spread. She continued the ruse. "Why do you suppose we built a fire on a hot day like this?"

"Why?"

"Why?"

"Scares 'em off. Makes 'em consider the fires of hell awaiting those who never brought themselves to repent for their sins."

Shug was concerned, "Like what sins, *specifically*?"

"Pride, greed, lust, envy, gluttony, sloth, anger …."

"Whew-w-w!" exclaimed Shug.

"Some folks for killin' and stealin'."

"Do lizards count?"

She didn't answer because not answering also forced them to think for themselves. She knew the old demons in this cemetery were slavery, abuse of power, infirmity, and wars.

A light breeze blew the smoke drift toward the group. Carmen pointed at it with a long straight stick she'd picked from the others.

She said, "See. There's one in anguish now. Hop back three times. See if the smoke rises or falls."

The cousins did as commanded. The smoke curled out, then drifted upward.

Carmen smiled, pleased with her performance. She took the Life Savers out of one pocket and placed one on each child's tongue like sacred wafers.

"Take one. You'll be protected. Looks as if we're safe for a spell anyway. But you kids oughta' keep that fire up."

The four cousins hustled to find debris to fuel the fire and begged Carmen to tell them a story.

With both fat arms, Bama clung to Francie's neck as she worked.

As wet leaves and water-soaked branches popped and hissed in the fire, Carmen reached into an apron pocket and pulled out small chunks of coal which she threw onto it.

Then she moved her body in an exaggerated rotation, like a witch watching over a boiling cauldron. She stopped. Her eyes rested on Bama and Francie.

With her voice in a deep foreboding tone, she told them that their grandfather had met the devil up here at this cemetery once.

"The devil!" they chorused.

"Listen carefully. I'll answer Shug's question by telling you a true story. True and scary," she said.

In broad daylight in the forgotten cemetery, the cousins became bewitched by her tale. They were afraid to get more than an arm's length from each other. One would dash off to get a limb or twig, then run back to the safety of the family circle around the fire.

Carmen's almost true storytelling prowess continued.

"One morning before daybreak, your grandfather, my father, was up here by himself. He'd left out for his deer stand an hour before dawn and decided to rest until his hunting hounds returned. So he leaned his rifle against a granite headstone— that one, I think—and sat down on top of it to rest a spell and to watch the train from Huntsville pull in and out of the station. Now that was about 1960, and he was getting on up in years by then. Maybe sixty or sixty-five.

"The way he told it to me was that he dozed off with his head leaned against his chest and his arms folded this way. (She showed them.) When he awoke, he started to reach down for his rifle and saw that a whopper of a rattlesnake had come up and wrapped itself around the gunstock.

"Now if it had been a small or even a regular-size rattler, I know your grandfather wouldn't have been one bit afraid to stomp his head into the ground and kill him. But as I said before, this was a whopper as big around as a man's arm and vile-lookin' with so many rattles he couldn't count them all.

"This granddaddy rattler was daring your granddaddy to move.

"Daddy, your Poppa, was mighty respectful of a rattlesnake that long. Tired and hungry, he had no desire to wrestle with the devil or a snake. He kept sitting and sitting, waiting for that rattler to spot a field mouse or lizard and move along about his own business.

"But he stayed put. My daddy told me the snake must have thought the gunstock was a log or tree trunk. He claimed it as his own personal property.

"Well anyhoo, after a lo-o-ng time, Daddy began rising off that grave marker a fraction of an inch at a time. Just an itty-bitty bit every five minutes or so.

"It took him two hours to stand up enough to run off. At the ballfield, he told the folks practicing there a braggadocious lie about the viciousness of the rattlesnake and the awesomeness of his bravery." Auntie shook her finger once at each cousin and continued, "Bragging in a cemetery is a sin by decent folks' accounts but not at sports. You'll never get past Saint Pete's gate if you're a braggart around dead folks. They'll tell Gawd.

"Anyhoo, he went back looking for it that very afternoon and bushhogged the cemetery so the devil would leave God's saints alone," she concluded.

Spellbound throughout, the cousins were relieved.

Her stories wove spells over them like no bound book or television show could do.

Shug asked how Poppa figured out the snake was one-in-the-same as the devil.

His mother continued roasting the wieners over the hot fire. As usual she delayed her answer, as if recalling an event stored so far back in memory it needed dusting and polishing before retelling.

"Why, Shug Jordan, my daddy said his proper posture never returned after that encounter. He walked stooped way over the rest of his life. It's true. I remember it clearly. His hair came in cloud white almost overnight. And children, let me tell y'all, those are two probable signs you've been wrestling in the devil's business," she concluded.

Although she was the oldest and smartest, Francie almost believed Auntie's story. It made sense, somewhat. She never could tell what parts of her stories were actual and what parts were made up. But always, like today, just the way she told them made each one believable.

Shug kicked a fire ant hill built upon the flat side of the headstone that his mother had pointed out as the place Poppa encountered the devil.

Red fire ants carrying gel-encased eggs scurried away frantically. Some crawled toward him, and he backed away.

"Git away," his mother demanded, giving him a shove.

"Just ants."

"Well, let me tell you, young man. Fire ants know. They followed hellraisers onto a cargo ship that landed in Mobile, Alabama fifty years ago and been causing Southerners in all ten states hell ever since. Haven't you noticed anywhere there's a bit of mischief kicking up, you'll find fire ants moving out to sting?"

"The highway!" Francie exclaimed. "That's why there are fire ant hills as big as tires at the edge of the new highway where the legs were found! Those were *bad* guys."

"If they're lined up east to west, it indicates dying. If the ant hills are lined up north to south, it indicates lying. Which way are they facin', Francie?"

"I don't remember."

"Well, well, young'uns. The fire ants know. They just know."

"You owe us a really scary story, Mother," fussed Shug. "One with blood, guts, and gore."

"Not today," was her reply.

"Tell us about the little girl and the donkey buried right there," Shug said, pointing to the only above-ground grave in the cemetery.

Rising about two-and-a-half feet above ground and long enough for a giant, it was made of tightly stacked flat fieldstone rocks, topped with an enormous sarcophagus-like slab of limestone with an indecipherable inscription. Who was inside was lost to the current generation yet commanded attention like an imposing statue in a battlefield.

"Well, Shug Jordan, that would be a Civil War story that took place in Chattanooga, called 'the battle above the clouds,' where sixteen hundred soldiers died. Blood, guts, gore a'plenty; but I don't feel like tellin' that one today," replied Carmen. "It's a slippery slope into criminal bragging when two sides are talking about the same battle. And just look where we're standing."

She asked about the hot dog buns. Francie remembered seeing them on the kitchen table. Both looked through the food supply and couldn't find the new package of buns.

"I know," smiled Carmen, good-naturedly. "Let's eat 'skint dogs' for lunch."

She showed the cousins how to eat a bunless wiener with ketchup dripping over it, which they liked even better. Shug yelped like a wounded dog. Little Bea squealed when ketchup oozed down her chin and onto her shirt. Fretfully, Arlo darted in and out among the messy children, licking the red stuff that dripped to the ground. Carmen did a little yelping too, to make the children giggle.

She took out pieces of note paper from one apron pocket and folded them into triangular cups. Francie poured Kool-Aid from a plastic milk jug into each paper cup, one at a time. Since leaving Auntie's cottage, the frozen juice had turned slushy, just the way they liked it.

Little Bea and Bama wanted to roast marshmallows next.

Carmen looked all around for the treat before deciding she'd forgotten the new bag of marshmallows, too.

She reached into one pocket and found six jellybeans, a small box of raisins, and three pieces of clove chewing gum. She gave the cousins their choice for dessert.

For the next half-hour, Carmen worked hard pulling beggar's weeds and Sweet William vines from the graves. She put Sevin dust on ant hills and sprayed insecticidal soap on Japanese beetles eating the leaves of antique rose bushes. Little Bea and Bama picked buttercups and black-eyed Susans to place beside each marker. Francie and Shug dragged large tree branches to a ditch.

By the time the sun began to dip behind the tall trees, Cemetery Hill looked more sacred than scary.

When the brush fire burned out, they picked up their belongings to head back and to pick blackberries along the way.

Carmen gave them a farewell reminder. "Whenever leaving a cemetery, you've got to fill it with love until next time. My granddaddy, your *great*-granddaddy, told me to always take a parting look over my left shoulder. That's the side closest to your heart. You can dust off a little love to leave until next time. So, I do."

The youngest generation of Kirwins marched down the southern slope of

Cemetery Hill dusting love from their hearts. Each glanced over their left shoulder, honoring a time and folks past, having feasted again on their family heritage of great storytelling.

Carmen knew there was no donkey from the Civil War buried in the above-ground grave in a Christian cemetery. It was a tale. The truth lay nearby because she knew that every generation of Kirwins had cared deeply for their domesticated animals.

Vividly she remembered coming up here with her granddaddy to bury Dan, one of a matched pair of Clydesdale draft horses. They repeated the family procession two months later when Molly, the other plow horse, grieved herself to death.

Throughout Carmen's lifetime, their beloved animals were buried at the far edge of the clearing and marked with surface-flush flat rocks only. Carmen knew they were there. And so did Rory.

Her glance over her shoulder was to her lifetime of much-loved pets. All were buried nearest the mulberry tree downhill from the humans.

Rory would come tomorrow to bushhog both cemeteries. Afterward she would scrub the granite and marble headstones.

To change the mood, she began singing a rollicking country song by Hank Williams, "Hey, Good Lookin'."

CHAPTER 10

Stealing, Lying, and Dying

"It's just the life for me," said Tom. "You don't have to get up mornings, and you don't have to go to school, and wash, and all that silly stuff. You see, a pirate don't have to do anything, Joe." "Oh, yes," said Joe. "I'd rather be a pirate, now that I've tried it." That was Tom's great secret: to return home with his brother pirates and attend their own funerals.

—MARK TWAIN, THE ADVENTURES OF TOM SAWYER

The journey home was long for Francie who, like Bama, was hungry again. The short trail from the cemetery to the logging road was a dense undergrowth of stinging nettles and briars that scraped her legs. She was glad she'd worn her heavy work boots.

After they descended the deep woods, they picked up the dirt logging road again and moved along faster.

A covey of quail scurried in front of them and into some wild honeysuckle vines.

Iridescent green ruby-throated hummingbirds sipped nectar from the throats of the honeysuckle blooms with their needle-size bills and tongues. They darted away at the quails' motion but quickly returned to the juice they needed to fuel their busy tiny bodies. Like drunken fairies, they flitted from fragrant bloom to bloom desperately seeking drink regardless of the presence of humans.

Because of a recent heavy summer rain, the logging road looked like a choppy sea of pine needles wadded together and washed downhill into ripple patterns. Fat pinecones dotted the now dry seabed like tugboats caught at low tide, askew until the next downpour pushed them along. Also exposed were shard-size pieces of petrified wood released from the bald earth where fossils were imprinted in the exposed rock.

Auntie pointed out deer and raccoon tracks crossing the dirt road when it had been muddy. They watched sparrows take dust baths by kicking up dry sand upon themselves, leaving whirligig imprints where they'd played.

The work today had been minimal. Francie regarded the summer outing as useful, but the 3:00 p.m. walk home would be the hottest of the day.

Francie breathed deeply. Shug was unusually quiet. Bama had fallen asleep on her shoulder. It was summer. *Time for kids to be kids and teenagers to be teenagers, not babysitters,* she thought.

Yet, Francie felt relaxed and at peace with herself. She refused to let her two main problems, the eye diagnosis and what to do about Opalee's bullying, enter her mind. She refused to think about Dad's many farm problems or the mystery of the dismembered body parts. She refused to think about the disruptions caused by the highway construction and the many changes Dad predicted were to come to their small hamlet.

Today she was enjoying being outdoors with Auntie Carmen. Even fifteen-year-olds enjoy getting dirty and sweaty sometimes.

Blackberry bushes along the edge of the logging road were ripe for picking. Blue jays darted overhead. One dive-bombed Little Bea's disheveled curls, and she cried out. The birds fussed at the humans as they approached their private vineyard.

"*Now,* Shug Jordan. *Now's* the time to shoot!" said his mother, filling the ammunition chamber of his air rifle with tiny pellets.

He cocked it and took aim at a blue jay and shot. Missed. The blue jays did not fly away.

He took another shot and missed.

Carmen took the gun from him and scatter shot a horizontal pattern into the tops of the bushes. The vines quivered.

All the blue jays flew away. Nearby, they watched their treasure being looted.

Carmen set the air rifle down away from the children.

She took folded lunch bags out of a lower pocket and handed one to each cousin. She cautioned sleepy Albert to stand close to Francie, who now needed both hands to pick berries. He was instructed to pick from the lower branches but to watch for snakes.

She moved Little Bea and Shug about five feet away and told them the same.

"Y'all pick twice as many blackberries as you eat, and we'll have enough for Vincent's welcome home cobbler," she said.

The tops of the wild blackberry's vigorous branches had been picked clean by a variety of birds who took the easiest pickings first.

Francie stretched to reach deep into the bush's thorny vines where every ripe blackish-purple berry grew almost two inches long and was bursting in plumpness. She hated thorns, but she loved blackberries!

She filled the bottom of her sack in five minutes and ate enough sweet berries to soothe the sharpest hunger pangs.

Little Bea and Shug ate what they could get to easily on the lower branches without getting stuck by the thorns. They picked in slow plucking motions, the way cotton is released from the boll using all fingers.

Carmen picked directly above the two. And fast! She filled her hand before dropping the plump blackberries into the empty gallon milk jug she'd slit open with her pocketknife. Her fingers were stained purple as she worked deftly.

The sun shone directly against Francie's back, but she didn't complain. Auntie handed her a clean handkerchief to tie around Bama's tender skin like a neckerchief.

Shug stopped to rest. He glanced at his air rifle.

"No stopping. This is quick work," his mother said, noting his disinterest.

"I can't. My stomach hurts," he moaned.

"Get up, son. Vincent's blackberry cobbler."

"Auntie Carmen, Shug looks green," said Little Bea, concerned.

His eyes were dark and deep set. He didn't look like he was faking. The nine-year-old fell forward on his hands and knees and began to vomit. When he stopped, his mother wiped his mouth with the corner of her apron and hoisted him onto her hip.

"Goodness, Shug Jordan, you're as light as a feather. Al Bama weighs more than you do," she said.

Shug leaned his head on her shoulder.

Realizing they would be headed directly home, Francie grabbed the flour sack of leftovers while Little Bea and Bama examined the vomit with sticks.

"It's hot, and I walk faster than y'all. May I walk ahead and get the first bath, Auntie Carmen?" Francie asked.

Her aunt said it was okay for her to go on ahead.

"More berries, please," requested Little Bea, who dropped her stick and picked up her sack.

Francie walked briskly. Troubling thoughts returned in an unorganized barrage. They darted about in her head like the mad blue jays. Anthills. (Was that an Indian warrior peering out from that tree?) Don't boast in a cemetery. Leave a little love behind. (Did a Union soldier scurry around the bend?) Vincent. Blackberries. Kimberlee. Supper waiting on the table. (Have deer hunters been shooting and cleaning deer in their woods out of season?) Mama being mad. Glenn. (Is a demon a sin or a person?) Shaving her legs tonight. The book she wanted to finish reading. Evil spirits passing right through you. Spirits possessing your body. So many places for murderers to hide out.

"A-r-l-o," Francie shouted. "Come on, boy."

She needed a friendly companion. She was dealing with a lot of unanswerable thoughts.

The dog could hear Francie, but he would not leave his mistress in her distress with the sick boy.

Plus, the dog and others knew but Francie did not know that Little Bea had tumbled into the blackberry bush and her curls had become entangled in the briars. The more she cried and thrashed, the more distressed Carmen became trying to untangle them. After several minutes, she took blunt school scissors out of one apron pocket and began cutting the tangled hair free from the briars.

"Arlo!"

At some distance, Francie stopped calling his name.

She could not see or hear the others.

A strange chill came over the creek trail she walked. She thought how in ghost stories they can fly straight through you. She needed something warm to wrap around her. She stepped even more briskly to get out of the dark ravine and nearer home.

An eerie stillness filled the creekside trail. A lone mourning dove called for his mate. A startled frog shrieked shrilly. Acorns fell loudly from tall oak trees into the water, *plunk*.

A single human shrill came from behind her.

Shug!

He was running as fast as he could toward her, whooping and screaming. The closer he got, she could see him flailing his arms about his face and neck.

Francie yelled at her cousin to stop.

He yelled something back.

As he passed her, Francie saw a swarm of thick, menacing gnats encircling his face.

Shug stopped, turned, and tried to talk. The miniscule black bugs flew into his mouth with such force that he choked. Others dive-bombed his nostrils or plastered themselves onto his eyelids. They landed by the dozens on his sweaty neck and ears.

Dropping everything, Francie swatted at the swarm of black specks with a limber pine needle branch, but they continued their relentless efforts to attach themselves to the boy.

Carmen came running ahead with Little Bea and Bama following far behind, both crying.

Carmen shouted, "Keep him moving, Francie. Get him into the creek."

Stumbling along, Francie dragged Shug down the embankment and into the creek. He jumped into it up to his knees and sat down in the water. The persistent swarm encircled his face like a tornado.

When his mother reached the creek, she waded toward him. She splashed water at the gnats. They dispersed and disappeared within seconds.

Shug spat out a mouthful of the dead pests. A tangled mass of wet blond curls framed his irritated skin. Carmen hurriedly unbuttoned his shirt and tried to take it off. It wouldn't budge. The shirt seemed glued to his body.

"What's going on here?" she exclaimed.

Shug cried and picked gnats out of his nostrils.

His mother straddled his legs to keep him submerged in the cold water and tried to force the shirt off.

"I just don't understand," his mother said.

Carmen tugged and twisted. "Hands up," she commanded her son as she gave a hard yank to pull off the shirt. When she did, she saw a frozen plaster of oozing marshmallows on his skin. She peeled the torn plastic bag away.

His skin peeled off with it. He cried out in pain.

"Marshmallows?"

"Our marshmallows!" exclaimed Little Bea from the embankment.

Shug explained sheepishly, "I was a pirate smuggling treasure on a secret mission. Maybe I ate a few, too."

Little Bea and Bama jumped in and tried to dunk him. Arlo jumped in and tried to save him. Francie splashed water in his face until they all were drenching wet.

Calmly Auntie Carmen pulled a half bar of Ivory soap out of her apron pocket and rubbed it on the marshmallow pasted onto Shug's stomach. He wiggled and squirmed. His three cousins flanked him, daring him to get up.

"Well, well, I reckon we'll just consider this our bath time," Carmen said, laughing good-naturedly, realizing Shug's crime was also his punishment.

She handed the soap to Francie, "You're next."

Francie soaped off underneath her clothes, handed the bar to her sister, and dove into the deeper depths to rinse off. She forgot about her eye patch.

She reached out her hands to touch the bottom. When she did, at once she sensed that what she was touching was not a smooth rock. It was soft, spongy, and with a shape that seemed to come apart.

She kicked off from the bottom with her boots and emerged, screaming hysterically.

Popping up directly behind her was the naked body of a dead man. She looked into his empty eye sockets and screamed until she lost her voice.

Auntie Carmen pulled her away and shielded the little ones from seeing the body. As soon as she could, she set them all facing away on the embankment while she tried futilely to pull the bloated corpse to shore.

But Francie *had* seen him. With both her eyes, she saw that his legs were missing and that his whole torso had been slit open, gutted as clean as crappie ready for frying.

The cousins did as Carmen demanded and faced away from the gruesome sight. Arlo swam to the other side and chased several deer up Arrowhead Mountain. The cousins recognized the shape walking from the springhouse toward them.

"Mama!"

"Auntie Laurice!"

Assessing the situation, she directed Francie to take the little ones directly home and for no one to look back.

She stepped barefoot over slippery rocks. She spotted and stopped to swoop up a perfectly knapped arrowhead point stirred loose in the silt from all the activity in the creek. She got as near Carmen and the waterlogged body as she could without going into the deep.

Carmen gave the human torso a shove to propel it toward her. Laurice got her arms under his arms and tugged gently as she stepped backward.

Carmen swam across.

They stood together staring down at a middle-age Black man's head, torso, and arms. He was missing both legs and internal organs.

"Oh, my Gawd! Laurice, I know him!"

"You do? How?"

"I can explain, but I don't want to."

"Well, Carmen, right now I don't care. Let's just call the sheriff," said Laurice.

"No!"

"No? Why?"

Carmen took the Ivory soap out again and began washing her hands, turning and rubbing them repetitively.

Near tears and with guilt in her voice and on her face, she explained that she knew the man from a nudist camp about two miles away on the eastern ridge. About a year ago, a nudist club discovered the site of the old convict camp that had been there in the 1940s. They'd been meeting there.

"You're a nudist?!" asked Laurice in disbelief.

"Only recently."

"Holy hell, Carmen," Laurice declared as she took the soap from her hands and began splashing creek water on them.

Carmen attempted an explanation.

"I heard mountain music from the backwoods and kept following it until I got near their camp. They are regular folks from all around the state. They meet at the convict camp on nice weather weekends."

She repeated, "They're regular folks, just like us."

"No, they're not!" Laurice stated as plainly as she could for a registered nurse who'd seen plenty of undressed patients in examining rooms.

"They are so free. They commune with nature that way."

Laurice retorted, "Well, one or two of them is dead and way down here on our property. How'd that happen?"

"I don't know. I do know him, but I don't know how they died."

"Sounds like a partial answer to me."

"It is."

"So …"

"I don't want to tell you," Carmen repeated hesitantly.

Laurice shot back, "You'll be telling plenty of law enforcement when you're in jail."

"I'm sorry, but I'm not guilty," Carmen said. "You don't think I could kill another human being, do you?"

Laurice sat on a log and put her hands under her chin. She wanted to get home to the children but obtaining this information from her sister-in-law came first. She grew more frustrated.

"Why were the two men here at Merrifield Farm, Carmen?"

Carmen took a resigning sigh and made the connection.

"This guy, Gus, would come back with me sometimes or meet me here."

"Here? Right here?"

"Yes. We both liked swimming nude."

"Here?"

"I said yes."

Laurice thought for a few seconds. "So, Jordan's sleepovers at our house were so you could have trysts with a nudist?"

"Yes."

"Damn it. I'm so mad at you right now! I've always trusted you."

"I know. I'm sorry."

"So, then it became a threesome? And where's the other body?"

"No. And I don't know. I said I'm sorry, but I'm not guilty."

They were silent.

Carmen said, "The other guy they'll find, if he's dead too. His name is Roland-something. He would wait up on the logging road to walk Gus back. They work at the same accounting firm in Decatur."

A stream of cuss words expressed Laurice's anger.

Then, "Well, just shit-fire! If you knew this two weeks ago, you've withheld information from the law. Rory's going to be implicated somehow; I just know it."

Carmen said, "I didn't know who it was until just now. The legs were covered or gone when I saw the commotion from atop Arrowhead. And how would I know if I had seen them? I'm innocent."

Laurice stood up, then gave Carmen a hand up from the log.

"Let's go face the music. Legal, not mountain music."

CHAPTER 11

Vincent Opens the Pasture Gate

Segregation now, segregation tomorrow, segregation forever.
—George C. Wallace, Alabama governor 1963-67, 1971-79. 1983-87

After things settled down at home, that is, after Carmen and Rory had gone to the Sheriff's Department in Ellisville and curious neighbors departed, Laurice made Francie a bed on the front porch swing.

She brought her the telephone after it kept ringing for her. Francie's school friends wanted to know one thing: What did a dead man's body feel like?

She admitted she had been scared at first. She was not ready to talk about the mutilated body.

Earlier, rushing from the creek incident to home, the children first dealt with Francie's eye. The soggy bandage had fallen off in the creek. She could see, but it was blurry and felt scratchy. Shug irrigated it with solution and squeezed eyedrops into it.

Then, they dropped their wet play clothes in the laundry floor and wrapped themselves in beach towels and cotton blankets. Francie applied ointment to Shug's chest. Silently they sat on the sofa, huddled together, until Bea spoke.

"What happened?" asked Little Bea. "Why were you screaming, Francie?"

"I thought I cut my foot on a piece of glass," she lied.

She would wait and let Mama tell them.

After about an hour of curiosity callers, Francie stopped answering the telephone altogether.

Her mother stepped out to check on her. "How's it going?"

"Fine, Mama, except I feel numb all over."

"You've had a shock."

"Why won't y'all tell me anything? I'm fifteen. Y'all made me stay in the house like one of the babies."

Laurice sat in a white wicker rocker across from her daughter.

She said, "I can only stay a minute. I left Shug and Bama in the back, getting their baths. I'll try to answer your questions unless I think it's more than you need to know."

"Fair enough. What's Auntie Carmen got to do with any of this?"

"She thinks she knows the two dead men from the highway construction."

"One was that dead guy in our creek?" Francie queried.

"Yes."

"Well, Mama, Auntie Carmen didn't kill them. I know that. Is that what they think?"

"Not yet."

"Oh."

Her mother assured her, "It will all get straightened out."

Francie complained, "It was an exciting murder mystery until our family came under suspicion. We're not bad people."

She was thinking of the stares and the gossip about her when school was back in session.

Laurice, who had been brushing her own hair during this exchange, finished pulling her black hair into a ponytail. She got up and began brushing Francie's thick dark-brown hair.

"Francie, I've learned that deep inside each of us is a part we don't recognize. It's there until someone else sees it in us. This shadow self is often ugly, like meanness or bigotry. Most of us can't face this truth; so, we tuck it back down and forget about it."

"Ouch! Too tight," grimaced Francie. "I don't understand what you're saying."

"My family didn't have an easy time in Birmingham. My father used to tell me, 'If you listen with smart ears, southerners will tell you exactly who they are.'"

"Like they're going to say, 'Hello, I'm Susie, and I'm a murderer? No way, Mama," commented Francie.

Laurice finished her daughter's ponytail, then turned her around to face her. It flashed across her mind that she was looking at her mirror image.

She said, "If someone says, 'I don't follow the rules,' then don't expect him to follow rules at sports or politics or rules of the road in traffic.

"If he brags that he got something for nothing, like cheating a man out of a day's pay, he's saying, 'I have cheated, and I'll do it again.'"

Information overload for Francie, whose response was, "Well, I still don't understand."

"You will one day, Francie."

"Mama, my eye is throbbing. Will the dead man's corpse gunk in the water make me go blind?"

"Get infected? No, Shug did a decent job irrigating your eye. We need to thank him. Your eye is throbbing because it's not quite ready to go back to work. Wear the eye patch at night and whenever it throbs. Let's go easy until next week's appointment, huh?"

"Sure, Mama."

Laurice stood up to go back into the house. She looked down at the teen version of herself. Her heart filled with love. She was no orphan lost to misfortune; she was Francie, Beatrice, and Albert's mother. She would protect them with her life. She kissed Francie's forehead, straightened the sheet over her, and took the telephone and its long cord back inside.

"Shug Jordan! Al Bama! Get back in the bathroom. You're dripping on my carpet! Don't make me get a fly swatter to your legs."

"Mama, ma-ma-ma, he hit me!"

"Did not! You pushed me."

Francie liked that her family members were acting normal. She liked the way their home held the sounds of activity.

She had heard the mail carrier stop to deliver their mail earlier, so she decided to walk down to the mailbox.

About halfway down the gravel drive, she encountered their neighbor, Ben Ludeke, cutting privet bushes along the fence line.

"Yoo-hoo!" he called out to her. "*Hallo.*"

She walked over.

Mr. Ben wore a frayed straw hat and a long-sleeved cotton work shirt. A sling blade rested against a fence post as he took a sip of water from a jug.

"*Guten Tag,* Ms. Francie," he greeted her. He set the jug down. "Has the mailman run yet?"

"Yes, sir."

"You are all right these days? Da eye, I mean," asked Mr. Ben in a German accent oddly mixed with deep South influence.

"Yes, sir. I'm not wearing the bandage until my eye starts hurting. I can already see out of it."

She caught a little movement to her side and turned her head to see someone little.

"Who's this?" she asked.

"Amado-somethin'. He's from somewhur down in South 'merica. Don't speak no English. And I speak no Spanish. A little German, maybe still. But we'uns are best buddies today, you see," said Mr. Ben.

Francie smiled and waved at the preschooler who had big brown eyes that twinkled back at her.

"Maudie's mite allergic to privet blooms."

"Yes, sir."

"Gotta work 'em regular, or they be spread like kudzu vines, you see. It's goldenrod for me. Sends mah allergies into fits."

"Yes, sir," said Francie again, knowing he'd positioned himself strategically to watch the sheriff's vehicles, ambulance, and ambulance chasers. "Mr. Ben, it's awfully hot outside this afternoon. You think you ought to be working so hard?"

After Mr. Ben's cardiac arrest, he had to let his farm go into a state of disrepair. His barn was crammed with rusting tools, tractors with flats, harvester combines years past warranties, and planters that should have been sold off years before.

Although weeds and briars had taken over his fields, he made sure he kept his shady front yard swept clean of any grass or weeds for Maudie, his arthritic wife, who feared snakes.

"Hard work never bothered me none, you see," said Mr. Ben. "Just ask anybody around. Ain't that rite, Amado?"

The boy smiled.

Mr. Ben dug his hand into his pants pocket to retrieve a handful of Fruit Loops.

"Watch dis," he told Francie.

He proceeded to hang pieces of the dry cereal on the cut ends of privet limbs, like Christmas ornaments.

Amado whacked at the base of the bushes with a toy plastic screwdriver. When the limbs shook, the cereal fell to the ground. The boy grabbed and ate them faster than Arlo gobbling watermelon.

"Darndest thing," said Mr. Ben, chuckling. "No take dem out of mah hand. Guess momma Bonita says no. But shure as chickens lay eggs, if turn my back, that little Mexican rascal would steal me blind."

Francie held back caustic remarks.

She asked about the migrant work force Mr. Pratt kept seven months out of the year.

"I leave 'um alone," said Mr. Ben, matter-of-factly. "That's whut Pratt told me to do. And that's the way it's been 'til this spring when he brought Bonita over. Said she could clean and hep out with Maudie if da little fella could come too."

Francie remembered the Hispanics Dumpster diving. She asked him if they liked vegetable soup.

"I dun-no, you see. They all thin as sticks, 'cept the short chunky ones."

Again, Francie held back caustic remarks, but it was getting harder.

Mr. Ben said, "Quite a commotion at yur place this afternoon."

"Yes, sir."

Mr. Ben took a long draw from his cigarette, tossed it, and extinguished the butt end into the dirt with his boot.

He questioned, "True it was a Black man?"

"He was an accountant."

"Don't matter. A Negro don't belong in these parts. I'd probably a kilt him mahself. For Maudie's sake."

"Ms. Maudie's sake?" asked Francie.

"For they be rapists or drug dealers, you see."

Francie's temper erupted.

"No! They're not!"

"Better safe than sorrowful."

"Good-bye Mr. Ben. I must go now. I don't feel safe around *you*," she stated flatly.

"What you mean, child?"

"You're of German descent, Mr. Ben. *All* Germans are *murderers*. Think World War I, World War II, the Holocaust."

"Naw, we ain't not. You see, that's why we got lucky out of dere," he said. Then he whispered proudly, "We're from Jewish stock. We *umgewandelt, er-uh-mm* 'convert' in this place, USA, you know."

Francie felt a little twinge of guilt, pouring on her accusations so harshly. She'd been brought up to respect her elders.

She continued, "Well, I probably shouldn't be around you because you *look* different than me. You're awfully short for a farmer, and your skin is a different tone than mine."

"You're Italian, child," he answered with a mocking laugh. "Or something else."

"And *your wife* doesn't speak English," Francie retorted. "And I'm not Italian; I'm American. And not Black. Or German. A-m-e-r-i-c-a-n," Francie looked around with her arms spread open. "And heavens to Betsy, there's enough room around here in this great big open county for different-looking people."

There was silence for a few moments. Life-changing moments of reckoning for the retired, lonely farmer who began to look within and see his own bigotry.

"*Quatsch*! I get what you're sayin. Dey're not all bad."

Francie interrupted by shaking her finger at him, "Nope. Stop. Think."

He corrected himself, giving the thumbs up sign. "*Most* are *gesetzestreu*."

"Right."

"I'm the same as Amado, a child, and even I can see that the boy is hungry and couldn't tell you that."

She continued, "There's a hungry little child standing in your own yard, and you don't notice? With you being a Christian convert, what should you do? Entertain yourself? Feed him?"

The farmer shrugged and said, "I'm old man. He's fun to watch, you see. I can take him inside now and get him some of Maudie's boiled okra."

He laughed at himself. "I'm telling joke. No okra. Maybe too old to change. But will try."

What Francie wanted to do was show him he could change.

Step one.

"Mr. Ben, have you ever eaten a taco?"

The stunned farmer recoiled, "Never! *Nie*! What is dat?"

"Ask Bonita to stop cleaning and to cook you some tacos tomorrow. I think you'll like to taste something different for a change."

"Taco! Taco!" smiled Amado as he reached for the old man's hand.

Just as Mr. Ben reached down and took the boy by the hand to go inside for food, the three of them heard the crunch of gravel. A vehicle turned onto Francie's driveway. They watched a cloud of dust rise fender high as the car came to a sudden stop close to them.

"Back up! Back up, dude, that's my cousin," came a voice through the loud car's music of "Saving All My Love for You" by Whitney Houston blaring.

"Vincent!" screamed Francie.

"Vincent! *Guten Tag*! young friend," said Mr. Ben with gusto.

They walked toward the car.

"Hello and gosh! I'm so glad to see familiar faces, y'all."

Hugs and handshakes went around.

Mr. Ben laughed and began to speak to the people inside the car.

"I remember dis boy, only dis high, always hungry. Would drink milk out of our cat's bowl. Must hide de bowl. He grows up so bigger always hungry, Maudie say, 'Hide da cat!'"

The other two passengers got out of the car. The driver was taller than Vincent and heavier. The African American wore military fatigues. The passenger was a petite Asian woman or girl, not as big as Francie. Vincent introduced them. Her name was Lin. His was Everett. They were engaged.

"Jeezus, ya are tall boy," exclaimed Mr. Ben with his face upturned.

Everett and Lin made eye contact with each other as if to say, "Where on earth have we landed?"

"I'm a *man* and a *soldier*," stated Everett, "Oh yeah, and I'm Black. Any comment on that, sir?"

"*Nie*. Do ya play basketball, tall soldier?"

"Yes, sir. I do. I get asked that a lot," he responded. He turned to Vincent. "Do you play basketball, tall soldier?"

They bumped shoulders good-naturedly.

Vincent informed Francie and Mr. Ben that he'd invited them to come to Littafuchee. Neither had ever been in the state of Alabama.

Hugs and handshakes went around again with the newcomers.

Francie admired Lin's yellow satin dress and embroidered handbag. Lin gave her the purse to examine. While they were talking, Mr. Ben continued his reverie about a much younger Vincent.

Speaking directly to Everett, Mr. Ben said, "When da Vincent, size of Amado here, he love my planter. Big piece of equipment I need. He put dried Rice-a-Roni down seed hopper thinking he was helping me plant he like rice. It not work ever since. Okay, okay I say, he *der bubi*, but next year he turns on orchard fan inside da barn and burn his arm here," he pointed to a place on his own arm. Then, "Show 'em your scar, still dere?"

"Yes, sir, right here," answered Vincent, pointing.

Everett entered the conversation and offered to look at any of Mr. Ludeke's farm equipment while he was visiting.

"You charge outrageous?" Mr. Ben asked, interested.

"Not a penny, sir. I'd be happy to help Vincent's neighbor."

"You and your girlfriend come together for lunch tomorrow," he said, winking at Francie. "We be having tacos. You like tacos?"

"You bet!" said Everett.

Lin smiled demurely, as she was vegan.

"Tell you what I now decide. You and friend come stay with us now. You see, Maudie and I have no children and *sechs* bedrooms. Little houses at the Kirwins. Many of people. Full houses."

"We couldn't impose upon you like that, sir."

Mr. Ben insisted, "Tomorrow you come for lunch. Bring your suitcases. We have tacos. Yum. Then we start the refix of farm equipment. Fair trade, huh?"

"Do it, dude," said Vincent. "Beats sleeping on the floor of Mom's porch in a sleeping bag with a million blood-thirsty mosquitoes."

The two newcomers looked at each other, thinking alike: *Is southern hospitality always forced upon you like this?*

"All right. We'll be there for lunch at least, sir."

Shug ran down the driveway as excited as a kid on Christmas morning.

"Vincent! Vin'!"

He jumped up on his big brother's back and grabbed his army cap. He started talking nonstop while patting the top of his brother's shaved head.

"We picked blackberries for you today. I picked most. Then there was a dead man in Talwa Creek. And then Mom got put in prison. Prison, Vin', imagine that? Can I go stay in the barracks with you now that Mom's in prison?"

Vincent was embarrassed his company was witnessing the animated show of affection and the very confusing flow of information.

As Shug was not about to get off his back, Vincent smiled and said to them apologetically, "Sounds like a normal day in Dixie County. Welcome."

"Come on Shug, let's walk home so we can unravel what you just said," he said as good-naturedly as any Kirwin.

To Francie, he asked, "Where's my mother?"

"Jail," was Francie's one word confirmation.

Heading toward the cottage arm-in-arm with her grown-up soldier cousin, Francie called out to her neighbor, "New and different. Way to go, Mr. Ben."

The old man smiled, waved back, and led Amado toward his quiet house with huge white columns in front and five unused bedrooms.

While Vincent and Everett unloaded duffle bags and Lin's small suitcase at the cottage, Francie and Lin sat in the small front porch's old caneback rockers. Tall canning vats, pressure cookers, and empty canning jars lined the wall. Carmen's acoustic guitar leaned against the stonework.

"Who plays?" asked Lin, pointing to the guitar.

"Our aunt. She's good. Late at night we can hear her through our bedroom windows. I like the way the sounds of the strings blend with the evening breeze. Kind of fills it up like. Sometimes the robins and mockingbirds sing with the music. Really. At those times, I imagine it's the sound of heaven on earth and Auntie's a singing angel," said Francie. "Puts me to sleep fast."

"So, she's a good person? Not a jail maker."

Francie laughed, "Yes, she's a good person, the kindest person in Littafuchee. She sings lots of sad songs at night, though. Wait until you meet her."

"Good."

"Good."

Vincent dropped the last load on the porch and sat on the top step. Everett sat on top of his bedroll as there were only two rockers on the porch.

Vincent said he hoped Lin could sleep at Uncle's house or Bama could and Lin could have his room.

Francie nodded *yes*.

Vincent spat into the yard. Then asked, "Well, why don't you tell me what's going on here."

Francie got up and sat beside him on the step.

"Oh, Vincent, things have been going from worse to Worstershire, as Dad says. It's the highway construction messing everything up."

She told him about the infighting in Littafuchee concerning the changes the construction made. The icehouse gone made the anglers mad. Which side got the ballfield was a hot topic button, as silly as that was.

She told him about his Uncle Rory's problems around Merrifield Farm and how he'd sold off the cattle.

Then she told him about the legs found at the edge of the roadbed near Talwa Creek and how they just keep digging up the new highway trying to find the bodies.

"One body now," she corrected herself.

She told him about Shug and the gnats and her washing off in the creek like they've done dozens of times except this time she dislodged a human body.

Reaching the end of her story, she heaved and said, "And that's how Auntie Carmen ended up in jail."

"Why?" asked Vincent.

"Because she knew both dead guys."

"That's not a crime."

"I know. I know. Exactly. How does all that work, anyway?"

"They're just asking her questions, getting her answers recorded. That's all."

"There's a little bit more."

"Yeah?"

"Let Dad tell you."

"Uncle Rory has enough problems around here. Is he okay?"

"Yes. I think so," said Francie, remembering his mantra, "a farmer never complains." He anticipates rain. He anticipates better crops. He does what he can with the situation given to him by God because a farmer with unflinching faith knows things will work out according to God's plan.

"Well, I'll do what I can to help him while I'm here. Everett will help, won't you, dude?"

"You bet. Glad to help for some decent food."

"Food!" Francie remembered. "It's ready, and I'll bet y'all are hungry. Come on over to the house. Auntie cooked already. Fried chicken and dressing."

"Great!"

"Just give me a second to get the congealed salad out of her refrigerator," said Francie, hopping up.

Everett and Lin had heard jokes about southern casseroles and congealed salads full of mayonnaise and other mysterious ingredients that combined could give a person food poisoning.

They grimaced at each other. *Save me from this experience.*

Fifteen minutes later, Laurice and Francie had the dining room table set and serving dishes on it.

The same two doubters were making noises like starving animals, digging into the spread of southern cuisine while the little ones picked at the food on their plates.

Starving sounds turned to moans of delight when they enjoyed their congealed salads made from Carmen's secret recipe using fresh strawberries, blueberries, and pecans from the farm. (Perhaps a shot of rum had been added.)

When Rory and Carmen returned, the whole group sat on the front porch lit by full moonlight. Carmen sat on the porch swing with Vincent, patting his arm constantly. Shug sat on his lap. Francie served the homemade strawberry shortcake with refills of sweet tea all around.

Everyone was home again. But unknowingly, Vincent had left the pasture gate wide open, so to speak.

CHAPTER 12

What the Barn Knew

By Anne Beatrice, Age seventy-eight, year 1981

A barn is alive. Morning. Midnight. Every season. Every year. Inside its stalls, it gestates, then gives birth. It protects from rain and gives warmth in winter. A barn takes in hay and grain, then gives it back to the livestock. It waits for the byproducts, and then it waits for the cleanup.

Once upon a time, every barn was in its prime, boasting of right angles, vertical poles, and horizontal lines. "Good bones," as those at barn-raisings said. Broad-shouldered across, a barn holds weight and volume to capacity without complaining. After decades, it swoons and creaks arthritic with age yet holds the same mass plus permanently retired farm life relics.

Wide barn doors open and close, but never silently, to milk cows, plow horses, show horses, 4-H heifers, and mules. Barn doors open necessarily for cowgirls, milkmaids, trainers, farriers, veterinarians, workers, owners, and children.

All are welcome. Once within its inclusive doors, humans and animals find the barn a womb of maternal care.

All are welcome to work.

My grandchildren are welcome to work and play.

CHAPTER 13

Wallowing in it

Life for my family was a real struggle, as it was for most in those farming communities.

—JIM NABORS, ACTOR, SINGER

The Kirwin's barn was a pole-built rectangular building two stories high, built at the turn of the century.

The lapboard exterior over the original rough-sawn logs had several coats of red paint peeling in curled layers. Seven-foot-wide wooden gates were on either end. The central corridor was about twenty-five feet across from stall to stall, of which there were seven, each with feeding trough. The center had packed dirt and sawdust floors. Stalls were given soft bedding of hay.

The eighth space on the front right was the feed and tack room. It had an elevated plank floor where a few bails of fodder and grain and feed mix in barrels were kept. Supplies of feedstuff in bags and food pellets for the catfish in the pond were stacked neatly. Ropes, pitch forks, shovels, water buckets, harnesses and bits, saddles, blankets, galoshes, rainwear, and salves were kept there also. This space smelled heavily of sweet grains and sweaty leather. It was used constantly with sharp reprimands to everyone to not leave the door open to hungry livestock and prowling wild critters.

Seasonal storage of loose fodder gathered from fields was hoisted into the loft from trucks through the second-story loft door, as were rectangular hay bales tied with baler twine. Field corn was loose in the corn crib, piled to the rooftop after harvest and scant by winter's end. An antique pump organ and a mule-pulled bull-tongue plow became permanent relics in the loft, hoisted through the loft door over fifty years before.

Folks accessed the huge loft area from inside the tack room up a spiraling set of wooden stairs that had been reinforced many times over with odd-sized pieces of wood. Barn cats loved hiding in the tight spaces underneath the stairs. These cats were regarded as essential workers inside the barn, keeping mice and rats away from the livestock's food supplies.

Upstairs on the loft's two long walls hung antique leather harnesses and saddles from past years when the Kirwins kept show horses. Horseshoes were mounted in random displays. Faded ribbons and black and white photos were thumbtacked to a corkboard in the loft.

On the main level, the rear barn gate opened to a wide corral.

Thunder, Carmen's Tennessee walking horse, had the front stall. From there he served as the uncontested attendant and overseer of daily activities around the barn and barnyard.

Before the highway construction, the Kirwin clan had direct access between home and barn. Now that was impossible.

Rory made them ride with him in the back of the pickup truck in a big loop, which took them down the service road, across the highway junction, and back onto the old two-lane highway.

Francie felt cheated by the new highway because the barn building and silo were just across the culvert within sight of their house.

This morning Rory had added a stop at the Gillivray and Gillery Feed 'n Seed to pick up Kimberlee. Ms. Vivian, her mother, sent along a batch of freshly baked chocolate chip cookies for the children.

At the Feed 'n Seed, Houston waved down Rory's truck as he was pulling out to tell him he would not be attending the incorporation meeting at Merrifield Farm the next week and his reason for it.

He told Rory to cancel the meeting because he thought it was premature.

"Why?" asked Rory.

"It doesn't hav-h the backin' rite now-wa," Houston said. "This is merely a crossroads community."

He went on to explain, "Folks arah plain suspicious."

"About what?"

"*You*, Rory. They don't trust you any morra. All of them nixxer-ahs showing up on your do-o-r-step and in your cre-e-k."

"That's all explainable."

"I hate to sayah it, Rory, but you've *changed*. We don't *have* to in-cor-po-rate. We d-o-n-'t *want* to. And w-e-u-n-s *never will*," said Houston.

"That's mighty puzzling, Mr. Houston, 'cause I feel like I'm the same man I was last week, last year."

Rory continued, "I'm sorry you won't attend. Your presence would be a strong sign of support. I hope Chip attends. He'd make a good mayor for us."

"Not g-o-i-n to hap-pn. Not my boy."

Speechless, Rory stared at him for several seconds before tipping his cap and pulling out.

But the conversation concerned him all day. Why had Houston suddenly changed his mind? It couldn't be over Vincent's visitors, could it? Gossip about other folk's news travels fast and never takes the straightest route, he remembered. He felt strongly the same as other Littafuchans – my family is off limits.

After an hour's play at the barn, Shug convinced Kimberlee it was snack time. She and Lin distributed the pancake-size cookies, two to each person there—Bama, Little Bea, Shug, Francie, Mr. Rory, and finally themselves.

Kimberlee found Vincent grooming a horse in the back stall of the barn. Coyly she suggested feeding him his cookie while he brushed the animal.

"Sure," was his answer.

Kimberlee began breaking off small pieces and placing them in his mouth, letting her slender fingers linger there. Subtly she edged around to stand between him and the horse, facing him.

"That's not a safe thing to do Kimberlee," said Vincent when their bodies were pushed together by the horse shifting.

She remained in that tight position. She put a larger piece of cookie on his lips and leaned in to take part of it with her teeth.

"Better be careful, girl," Vincent said after swallowing the piece without chewing it.

"Why's that, pretty boy?"

"Emory here's a bit skittish. He threw Francie yesterday."

"Yeah? Well-uh, you se-e-em to be the skittish one. You ain't afraid of me, arah ya?" she said, tossing her long auburn locks to the side and striking a pose with her back arched and her chest uplifted.

"Kimberlee, you're a child. You are Francie's best friend. I respect you."

"Oh, poo! Don't respect me. Kiss me. You know I've always loved you."

"No! Just no."

He threw the brush down and led the horse out the back gate.

He called out a parting shot. "Besides, you're not ready for what I'm thinking about."

He took the horse to the corral and released him.

Even from that distance, Vincent tasted her fingers and felt their light touch upon his lips. His breathing was shallow. He began perspiring. Other things were happening, too.

Why did being around her make me feel like I was having a heart attack or something? he thought.

"Why does being around that filly make me feel like I'm having a heart attack?" he asked his Uncle Rory a few minutes later as they sat on the corral fence together.

Rory smiled and said, "She's too young for you. Still in high school."

"I know."

"She's Francie's best friend. There's a lifetime of complications in that."

"I know."

"You're at the age everybody's pairing up, son. It's natural. But know this, she ain't leaving Littafuchee. Her parents and grandparents will see to that."

"Well, that could be a real problem, Uncle Rory."

"How so?"

Vincent hemmed and stammered, getting around to what he'd vowed he'd tell his uncle while on leave.

"Well, sir, you see. The military and all. Littafuchee is where my family is. Not that I wouldn't come see y'all a lot," said Vincent with his head down, feeling as bad as the news he was giving his uncle.

"Uncle Rory, I know you need me around here, but I just gotta stay in the military as a career. I can't live out my life here," said the Army private.

No words were spoken for a while. Rory whistled softly. The young colt, Emory, approached and nuzzled him.

Eventually he asked, "What's the world got to offer you that you can't find over the mountain here? I need you at Merrifield Farm, son. I'm asking you to do your time and then come home."

"I've kinda made up my mind, sir. Maybe I can be here for planting season."

"Ummm," Rory mulled aloud. "Francie is so small, she's not much help with the heavy lifting. Lord knows, she'll stay right in there; but realistically, she's not the answer."

Vincent said, "Shug is nine. In a few years he'll get big like me. He'll help you."

"Ummm," said Rory, pondering. "What if you finish your military service and then come home and be mayor of Littafuchee?"

Vincent laughed. He grabbed his ribs and continued belly laughing. The colt bolted for the other side of the corral.

"Where'd that come from, Uncle Rory?" he asked.

"Let me play with the idea that you are not going to like it out there for long. We're starting to talk about incorporating Littafuchee before one of the larger municipalities annexes us. Good idea, right? We'd have a first mayor, then you. A Gillivray-Kirwin dynasty. Perfect!"

"Uncle Rory, sometimes I think you're as much a dreamer as Mom," smiled Vincent. "I don't know. I'm nineteen. I don't know."

Everett showed up where the heart-to-heart discussion was taking place beyond the children's earshot.

"There y'all are! I've finished for the day with Mr. Ludeke. Thought I'd stop by. See if I can help."

"Sure," said both men in unison.

"Wanna be mayor?" Vincent asked, laughing.

"What? No!" replied Everett. "I want to be a farmer."

They hopped down and strolled over to the water vats. Everett had taken to following Rory everywhere. He asked dozens of questions about how things worked on the farm. Rory answered them.

He was put to work mucking out the stables.

At the barn with their juice boxes in one hand and cookie treats in the other hand, the children had climbed upon the front hinged gate, two on one side, three on the other. Each wrapped an elbow around the open railing to hold on while Francie pushed gently against the barn with her foot to swing the gate open. From the outside, Kimberlee pushed with one foot, sending the gate back in Francie's direction. The barn gate seesawed back and forth slowly carrying its heavy cargo.

They chatted as they ate their cookies. Kimberlee kept an eye out for Vincent who was at the water vats with Mr. Rory in a discussion she had no idea included her future also.

She forced aloud a topic sure to impress her soldier boy.

She began midsentence, " …'n the boat capta-i-n sed Dad-d-ie-s marlin was the big-gest o-n-e-e he'd ever s-e-e-n."

Shug asked what a marlin was.

"A gigantic fish," Kimberlee answered simply.

"Like a thark?" asked Bama.

"Oh, no," said Kimberlee, leaning back, waiting for Francie to push off to make the gate swing with more force. "At least I don't a-think so. You tell him, Francie-e-e."

Francie didn't know exactly what a marlin was either, although she'd been to Gulf Shores with Kimberlee's family several times.

She stalled for a reply.

"Well (chewing), it's a marvelous fish with large fins and gills (swallowing). Haven't you ever heard of their magnificence? (chewing, then swallowing) Some are monstrous in size and mighty muscular too."

"Wow!" exclaimed Bama. "I wan'a catch one o'dos."

Francie and Kimberlee giggled.

Francie spurted a long alliterative line, "Marvelous, mysterious, marine marlin's mates make mere men's minds more mortified."

Skeptical of Francie's expertise, Shug yelled, "You're the liar this time, Francie. I just know it. I told Mom you made things up just to get me in trouble."

"Do not."

"Do so," said Shug, who was on Kimberlee's side of the barn gate.

He kicked the barn wall and sent the gate banging closed.

Thunder grew anxious over the children's antics. He began to whinny and pace in his stall.

In return, Francie kicked hard from her side. The barn door pivoted on its rusty hinges in the opposite direction. It sailed out over the manure-covered ground in front of the gate where cattle had stood waiting to be let inside the barn. Walk boards had been laid down over the area to access the barn.

Francie screamed loudly, "You don't need any help getting into trouble!"

"Prove it, you ugly heifer," chided Shug, kicking harder.

"You prove it isn't so, baby's butt," said Francie smugly.

Like Mr. Pratt's quick-tempered bull, Shug's temper flared. "I say you're lying! There isn't even such a thing as a marlin. That's a stupid name for a fish."

Snap! The hinges broke. The top one ripped out of the hinge plate, then the bottom one, toppling the five children into a heap on the mushy ground.

Lin, who had been inside petting the cats, jumped up and went to help.

Kimberlee began to tear up. Her green shorts set had clumps of manure smeared on its front and back. Francie tried to help her up. Oozy dung trickled down their legs and into their tennis shoes. It smelled awful. They smelled awful!

Shug had landed flat on his back. He didn't move for a few moments, then he looked at Francie with a hateful expression. He pulled himself up and trudged, limping, over to one of the freshwater vats. He fell backwards into it causing water to cascade out the low end.

Bama and Little Bea clung to the broken gate at the wall. Because they'd been topside, they had escaped most of the muck. Bama held his juice box in the air to keep it clean as Francie boosted him up the outside ladder that led into the hayloft. Then, she helped Little Bea.

"Stay up there until I come get you," she told them.

The little ones taken care of, she turned her attention to Kimberlee.

She was covered in it. She had to swat to keep the horse flies away from her face and hair.

"Oh, just look at my new clothes," she said, fretting.

Francie led Kimberlee around the side of the barn where the attached shed housed three tractors, a rototiller, bush hog, plus other farm implements.

At the corner of the shed, a rain barrel held water used for washing hands and equipment.

The girls stripped down to their bras and panties. They dropped their clothes into the rain barrel to soak. Francie poured water over their hair, arms, and legs. After they rinsed, they put on their dripping wet clothes.

Francie heard her father's truck crank.

Frantically the girls fished their tennis shoes from the barrel and scampered up the shed roof and into the hayloft from the backside, hidden from the guys' view by the silo.

Rory backed his truck up to the barn and got out.

He said, "Okay, boys, you can start unloading the four-by-fours under here. And put the six-by-sixes in front where we can get to them first."

"Yes sir, Mr. Kirwin," said Everett, eagerly.

Kimberlee continued to fret. Her makeup had washed off. Her hair was matted. She didn't want Vincent to see her clothes smeared with brown stains, much more how she must smell. The two teenagers hid in the hayloft with Bama and Little Bea.

They watched through the cracks in the plank floor, giggling softly and dropping straw down through the spaces on top of Rory below.

Rory had moved the broken barn gate so Vincent could get the truck inside.

"What on earth's happened here?" he said aloud, "Bet it's going to involve Jordan."

Not to be outdone by the falling straw, he teased the girls by threatening to send Everett and Vincent up to the loft.

"Wait a minute on that box of nails, Vincent. I may want you to put it up in the hayloft," he said.

He was grinning ear-to-ear.

Kimberlee squirmed under the loose straw to hide.

"Now, let's see …," Rory pondered aloud, scratching his stubbly chin. "In the loft or not?"

"Not!" called out Kimberlee in a strong whisper.

The guys nudged each other. They could see movement through the spaces between boards.

"You tote it, Everett."

"Naw, you do it, man."

Vincent picked up the heavy box of nails.

"D-a-d," plead Francie in her whisper voice.

With a sudden change of heart, Rory took the box of nails from Vincent.

"Nope. Let's get the outside corners reinforced first. When it gets too hot, we'll move inside."

"Yes, sir, Mr. Kirwin. Thank you, sir," said Everett.

Vincent patted his friend on the back and said, "And who says the good old country boys are the dumb ones?"

Everett's enthusiasm was unstoppable. "This is great, man. I mean, sir. I love it here. Uh-uh, well, uh…."

It was Rory's second time in twenty minutes to wait for a young man to put into words what was in his heart.

Eventually Everett managed. He said, "Mr. Kirwin, I was just, well-uh, you know, wondering …."

"Better wondering than wandering," teased Rory. He patted Everett on the back. "Just go ahead and get it out there. Do you want to ask me for Lin's hand in marriage?"

Everybody laughed, even Lin, who was usually as quiet as the cats.

Everett said, "I've done a lot of wondering. I'm two years older than Vincent. And, well, I just keep thinking what a beautiful place this is, Littafuchee, I mean. And all you guys too, of course. But, um-m, well …."

"Is this conversation going anywhere, Everett?" Rory asked.

Lin inched in close beside her fiancé. They had discussed what Everett was about to ask.

"What I'm trying to say is, I want to buy land here. Settle down in Littafuchee after I serve my time in the military. What do you think about that?"

"I think it's a fine idea. Good for a young man to think about his future."

"Well, um-m, Lin and I plan to be married when I get out in two years. Maybe before. This place feels like the missing part of me to me. Lin feels the same. I don't want to live in Chicago anymore. I want this. What you have. What Vincent will have. Would it be expecting too much from the white people here to accept a Black man and his family into this community one day?"

Rory remembered Houston's strange behavior earlier about incorporation. Was this the reason? Had Everett asked this of anyone else?

He thought deeply and carefully before speaking. "You know what you'd be up against? Folks distrust all outsiders, even whites. And there are only a few Black families anywhere in this county. Those good folks are well-known and trusted as generational families. They live near the railroad tracks near the county line and stay to themselves mostly."

"I'll introduce myself to them, sir," assured Everett.

Rory continued with the reality of land acquisition in the Littafuchee valley area. "Even whites fall under suspicion. I know a white real estate developer from Birmingham who has been trying for the better part of five years to buy a large tract of land here for residential development. No one will budge."

"You're saying it's impossible?"

"No. I'm saying at some point someone will have to sell. I hope it's to you, Everett. I like you. You're a diligent worker. You've got that military discipline thing going for you, too."

Everett absorbed Rory's meaning in a few seconds. "I understand. Thanks, sir. I'll get back to mucking, sir."

"Nope. Let's unload this first."

"Yes, sir."

They turned their attention to the barn's structure, measuring a sagging load-bearing wall in the back corner.

Cold and wet, Francie snuggled down deeper into the loose straw. She loved the smell of fresh hay and its muslin-like crispness.

She built a headrest of it and lazily studied the diagonal shafts of light splaying through the nail holes in the Dutch style tin roof. Dust particles drifted across the thin shafts of light like busy molecules she'd watched on school science films.

Odd pieces of antique furniture and equipment were stored in the loft. A pump organ, a spinning wheel, a chifforobe, a corn sheller attached to a wooden bin, a scythe, and a rusted washtub with scrub board filled the farthest corner like a museum of pioneer artifacts, never to be used again but valued for the services rendered before modernization.

She hoped someday Dad would paint a painting of it that captured the aging beauty of the loft's treasures. It should be a monochrome of dusty browns and grays with cherished objects fading into the distance like the passage of time. On the horizontal hand-hewn beam would roost beady-eyed gray barn owls, just as they were now, studying the juvenile intruders with intellectual curiosity.

Glancing at the wooden gate discarded on the burn pile, Rory said, "The old gal's gotta be replaced. Let's get galvanized steel. Vincent, go back into Ellisville and get two gates if they have them."

While he was measuring the barn gates' openings, Kimberlee scampered from under the hay.

"I'm coming!" she yelled out. "Vin-cen! Vin', wait!"

"Don't go, Kimberlee. Don't leave me here. They're sleeping now. I can't go," pleaded Francie.

Kimberlee's mind was set on Vincent and seeing as much of him as she could. She would make him like her. She would figure out how to do that. She scampered down the stairs to the main level just in time to ride with him. She did not forget to shut the tack room door securely.

"I'll ride with you, or you can drop me by my house," she said, twisting her long curly locks around her fingers. "I must look awful, though."

Vincent studied her fresh face and thought how much more appealing she was minus the heavy high school makeup. She had long legs that ended at her short-shorts.

Suddenly he wanted to kiss her.

Lin knew the horse they called Thunder didn't appear happy with all the activity. He was agitated that the barn gate was missing, and humans were yelling, so he continued to whinny and nod his head in that direction.

"Yes, it's gone," she soothed him by rubbing his soft warm muzzle. "I see it's different. I do. It'll get replaced before dark."

Only Thunder and the old wooden barn had heard correctly what all had gone on throughout the day. Smart horses and aged barns keep conversations private.

"Sh-h-h-h. Good boy, Thunder."

CHAPTER 14

More Law than Grace

*Community is and must be inclusive. The great enemy of community is
exclusivity. Groups that exclude others because they are poor or doubters or
divorced or sinners or some different race or nationality are not communities;
they are cliques—actually defensive bastions against community.*

—M. Scott Peck

Carmen was "out of jail" four days before she was ousted from Remnant Church for the second time.

The first time was ten years before when it became obvious that she was pregnant out of wedlock. A vote of members in good standing removed her name from the membership role. Asking for forgiveness for the sin of adultery before the congregation broke her spirit and protected the guilty. Tears flowed. All felt her redemption was earned.

Hands laid on her by the deacons and pastor reestablished her membership in Remnant Church just in time to begin rehearsals for the Christmas cantata. She played a pregnant Mary and sang solo parts in Bach's *Magnificat*.

Nightly Carmen prayed for the bitterness in her heart to be removed for that rejection. It was an unreported rape.

This time the church voted her out at the beginning of the eleven o'clock service. She exited the building as a middle-aged woman with no shame on her conscience and with no intention of begging a church full of self-righteous sinners for their forgiveness.

Being the Sunday for Holy Communion, all sinners were asked to exit, preserving the sanctuary for the chosen remnant.

Exiting through the double doors went a parade of code violators of what this independent church considered the cost of purity—no alcohol use, no tattoos or body piercings, no divorces, no long hair on males, no members of the Masonic temple, no adulterers or fornicators, or members who tithed less than 10 percent of their gross income.

There was a last chance altar call to ask for forgiveness for any other improper transgression against the Ten Commandments or Jesus's teachings. No one came forward. Also called to the front were those who might have *thought* they'd sinned. All these exclusions should have emptied the pews in the stained glass sanctuary entirely but did not. Pride trumped honesty once again.

Most departed for their homes or grandparents' homes. Others sat or stood around outside where the baptized among them would receive Holy Communion outside the sanctuary, thus preserving the chosen remnant inside.

The pastor's son, Trey, exited with the flow of folks. Only he and his parents knew the reason was that *he* was homosexual. Since coming out to his parents, the tenderhearted youth had been in intensive counseling with his father. The father-pastor prayed fervently to remove Trey's confessed sexual lust for the same sex while showing him provocative pictures of girls his age.

Several afternoons, the ladies at the Sheer Success Beauty Emporium witnessed the preacher tie his son to the foot of the cross in the church yard for hours at a time. The preacher lay prostrate on the ground in front of him praying.

Ladies in hair curlers and tin foil wraps watched an abominable misuse of the Abraham story in Genesis unfold. On that they agreed among themselves. However, because of their complacency and the church's structure, none of the women felt empowered to confront the pastor.

"Take my errant son, if I have offended you, heavenly Father," he had prayed at the foot of the cross only the day before. "Else purify his heart; set his mind in Your Word only, dear Gawd."

The traumatized and confused twelve-year-old had been counseled that "lust in your heart" is sin.

Today, church ladies with perfectly coiffed hair, perfectly heterosexual children, and Holy Bibles opened to scripture wrestled silently with their moral dilemma as they remained seated and quiet when the boy passed.

Two deacons accompanied the members of the judged just outside remnant-qualified to administer the consecrated bread and wine like pious missionaries to lepers.

Earlier before church service began, Everett and Lin had not been permitted admittance into the sanctuary although Mr. Ben tried to convince the greeters that both were Christian missionaries from Africa. "Others" were not allowed inside, they told Mr. Ben. He tried confusing them with his broken English, but they remained steadfast, redirecting them to a Black church thirty-five miles away.

Francie was proud of the retired farmer who welcomed Everett and Lin into his home, took meals together, and had lengthy conversations in their living room about each other's interests. She was convinced he had genuinely accepted the couple as equals.

The couple sat with Carmen on the church stairs, listening from the open doors. Their eyes exchanged unspoken words of disbelief in this church's rules.

Although Wyatt Hugg covered his tattoos for regular church attendance, folks knew they were there, so he always went outside with the church's marginalized Christians for communion.

With his wife and his children inside, he motioned for Everett to slide over so he could sit beside Carmen.

"How's about a Hugg?" he asked.

She did not like his humor or him.

He whispered to Carmen, "I know'd you didn't do it, Ms. Carmen. It was prob'bly one of the elbow boys. They's filled with putrid hate and conning evil."

She shushed him. "I'm listening to the music."

> Let us break bread together on our knees,
> Let us drink the cup together on our knees,
> When I fall on my knees, With my face to the rising sun,
> O Lord, have mercy on me.[4]

Wyatt had no self-control. He leaned over again and whispered, "But if'n weren't dem, Gawd-a-Mighty, somebody growing marijuanic in dem woods and got caught. Got kilt. Makes sense, huh?"

---

[4] African American spiritual.

"Will you leave me alone!" Carmen said loudly enough the others could hear. "I'd rather be dragged by a moving train down a railroad track than sit next to you."

"Mrs. O'Rourke, is everything all right?" Everett asked as he stood up and towered over Wyatt.

Carmen and Wyatt both stood up.

Wyatt exclaimed, "Jeezus, you're big, boy!"

"I'm a man and a soldier. I am Black. Do you have any problems with that?"

"Stop trying to intimidate me."

"Let's step out into the parking lot to continue this conversation in private."

Wyatt whispered "bully" loud enough to be heard and stepped aside. Everett sat back down next to Carmen.

As church service was concluding, Carmen went to the top of the stairs and waited so she could catch Jordan and Vincent on their way out.

When she saw them, she was overjoyed. She had two fine Christian sons. The three of them planned to spend the afternoon fishing at the lake.

Once outside in the parking lot, the Kirwins gathered in their small clan. Rory counted heads as he was prone to do. He lifted Little Bea and teased her about her new haircut that he called the briar patch pixie. Bama squatted close to the ground trying to catch a doodlebug. Shug joined him.

Francie whispered to her father, asking permission to walk home.

"Sure, Ponytail. We'll be leaving soon. I want to check in with a few fellas about the incorporation meeting, then I'll be on my way. Stay on the road. We'll catch up with you and pick you up, he answered, repeating, "Stay on the road."

Little Bea and Shug asked to go with her.

"No way!" Francie protested.

"Please."

"Please, please, please."

It was Rory who finally said that Shug and Little Bea could go and that Francie was in charge.

Before setting out, Francie went to the truck, sat down, and took off her nylon stockings that she'd worn to church to hide the scrapes and bruises on her legs from a bicycle wreck on their driveway's loose gravel. She and Little Bea left their purses and Bibles in the truck.

"Come on," she signaled to her young charges.

Little Bea took Francie's hand and pulled her along narrow Plank Road. They waited for a car to pass, then the three of them ran across.

Their house was about a mile and a half from the church traveling the newly asphalted service road that now had a sign "Kirwin Lane" for the postal route.

A shorter route would be cutting through Mr. Pratt's pasture and Mr. Ben's yard. Francie decided to try it. She stepped down and over the ditch toward the fence line and pasture gate.

"Francie! Come back!" shouted Little Bea from the shoulder of the road. "We're going to get into trouble. Mama will be mad again."

"No way she'll find out," Francie explained. "We'll be home before those windbags get through talking."

"I'm not going," Little Bea said. She glanced back in the direction of the church. "Mr. Pratt hates children."

"Well, count me in!" Shug exclaimed.

He hopped over the gate.

Francie threatened to tattle on Little Bea for eating out of the ice cream carton unless she came along with them right then.

"This is not what you agreed to, Francie. You know that. You told Dad you'd walk the road," Little Bea said.

"I can change my mind because I'm a leader, not a follower," Francie shot back. "Mama says that all the time, so come on."

Little Bea reminded her big sister that what Mama had said was that Francie will either be a great leader one day or serving jail time.

"Like my mom?" asked Shug from the other side.

"No. She didn't go to jail. She went *to* the jail, stupid, to talk to the investigators. Your mother is no criminal," repeating Vincent's words from four days before.

Francie put her foot on the lower strand of barbed wire and lifted the middle one for Little Bea to climb through.

Little Bea looked at her sister guiltily. "But we're about to break Daddy and Mama's rule."

Frustrated and angry, Francie squeezed Little Bea's hand until she cried out in pain. Her fingers turned white. Francie realized she'd just shown her own dark side. Hurting someone did not feel good, but she pushed her sister on through the opening.

By this time, the adult conversation taking place under the shade trees in the church parking lot had cycled back around from incorporation to the highway construction and, as of yesterday, the second recovered body. Carmen was left out of the conversation deliberately. Whenever the words Negro or darky were used, it was whispered.

She knew she was being gossiped about, but she knew her place in heaven was secure.

Laurice transferred day-old bakery products and other grocery items from the church ladies to contribute to Carmen's three dozen quarts of soup mix.

Into Carmen's old beat-up van went the donations.

Carmen and Laurice had planned to drop off this food to the migrant workers. As a second thought, Carmen asked Lin if she wanted to ride with her. She accepted.

The young cousins set off across Pratt Peterson's land, a flat, rolling expanse of lush green pasture grass. Although she wore her new glasses, Francie couldn't see into the distance where the property line ended and where Mr. Ben's expansive front yard started.

A herd of about two hundred dairy cows grazed peacefully under a small stand of shade trees in the middle of the pasture, not paying attention to the little humans' intrusion. To reduce the calving season, Mr. Pratt kept one bull among them.

Little Bea and Shug ran ahead of Francie. They played kick-the-can as they walked north through the bucolic landscape toward their home.

Across Kirwin Lane sat the work trailer for the highway construction crew. Inside on Sunday, engineers and superintendents stood around a slant-top table talking. The parking area was empty except for three trucks. Workers had Sundays off.

During the week, large groups of road crew hung around the trailer to clock in and out. It was they who had provided the litter that dotted both sides of the road.

During the school year as the cousins rode down to catch the school bus in the mornings, they'd watched those construction workers harass Mr. Pratt's migrant workers. They worked the massive fields east of the pasture. But often before daybreak, they were out scavenging in the commercial Dumpster beside the trailer or seen picking blackberries and wild onions that grew on the right-of-way.

Outnumbered, the migrants endured the crew's humiliating taunts. They kept at their task of sifting through discards and gathering food. They stayed in substandard cotton shacks on Mr. Pratt's property closer to the river or in their own portable housing. Otherwise, they kept to themselves, rarely venturing anywhere except to the gas station.

By late September when the crops were picked clean, they loaded up and moved along somewhere else.

Francie hardly ever thought about them throughout the school year until the next spring when their caravan arrived. She had never talked to a single Hispanic person except Amado.

Today was too hot for late June. Too humid to enjoy being outside. Too humid to think. Too hot to exert oneself. The longer Francie walked in the heat, the darker her cotton sundress became wet with perspiration.

Little Bea's long red gingham dress Auntie Carmen had hand-smocked for her stuck to the back of her legs as she walked ahead.

Shug's church clothes were a rumpled mess even before he arrived at Sunday school, but that was not unusual. His mother claimed he was a magnet for dirt and wrinkles. His hair was stuck to his scalp like bobby pin curls. A sweat necklace defined his collar.

Francie took the stick of chewing gum Glenn had given her at church out of her pocket and began to unwrap it. She thought about him for a few seconds. He didn't used to go to church. Was he doing it for her? Would he stop going if she did? She wanted to protest Auntie Carmen's ouster some way.

She stopped once to pick native oakleaf hydrangeas that grew everywhere this time of year. Their ivory cone-shaped clusters were as abundant as the purple wisteria that grew up trees and telephone poles in the summer, too.

Walking was better, Francie decided. At least that way, a little breeze could be felt.

Shug had run up ahead past the ceremonial Native American mound Mr. Pratt kept fenced. He was headed toward the lake. Easily distracted, he took a dried grass reed and began to prod for bugs hiding in the pasture grass.

"Hurry up, girls," he called. "It's scorching. I'm gonna have a heat stroke out here."

He raked the muddy straw across Little Bea's legs as she walked by.

"Don't! Yucky!" she cried out, running from him.

"Stop it, Jordan," warned Francie with delegated authority.

He retorted, "Who are you to tell me what to do, Bossy Betsy?"

"Leave her alone, bug brain."

"Heifer."

"Toad."

"Sissy."

What a pest! she thought. Francie wished she'd stayed in the truck and waited for her parents no matter how long they'd talked.

"Watch this," Shug said to Little Bea. He discarded his dress shoes and Sunday dress pants as he ran toward the oval-shaped lake, which covered about three acres.

Francie yelled out, "Stop, Jordan. You can't go in Mr. Pratt's lake."

"Why not?" he called out defiantly, continuing straight toward it.

"Well, because it's Sunday and because Mr. Pratt hates children," Francie warned.

Shug continued toward the lake in his underwear, T-shirt, and dress shirt.

Little Bea watched him and wished aloud for her swimsuit.

Francie called out to her cousin louder than before, "Go ahead, doofus, I dare you. Take off your good shirt, though."

Shug peeled off his shirt and dove into the shallow end of the lake.

Francie reached down and grabbed Shug's clothes.

"Let's hide them," she said to Little Bea.

"That's not nice," said Little Bea, wading into the water in her dress shoes.

Schools of minnows and tadpoles scooted into the darker depths when Francie entered the lake. She had hidden his clothes so that he would never find them under thick wild hydrangea bushes. She wore a smug expression. Besting Shug made her day.

The shoreline was murky as they followed it along. A scattered mix of wet feathers and down had been pushed to the edge. It was a favorite spot for wild birds and waterfowl. Watching the humans with wary eyes, a long-legged egret took to flight, dropping the small bream in his beak.

"Having a fun time, Shug?" Little Bea asked.

"I'm hunting some slimy frogs for you. Oh! A snake," he said before diving under.

"I've got one!" he called out gleefully.

The sisters took off running, leaving him and his clothes behind.

When the sisters neared the curve of the lake nearest the back fence, Francie heard a glass bottle shatter against a fence post. Then she heard a strange, grunting sound and turned to see a huge black bull charging toward them.

"Run, Bea!" she screamed.

Francie took off running. From behind her, she could hear the grunting sound get closer. She felt the ground beneath her feet vibrate from the startled bull's solid mass.

The raging beast could spear them with his long horns if he got close enough. He could run them down and kill them if they tripped and fell.

Francie noticed Little Bea's escape slowed by her water-soaked, patent leather shoes slipping on the grass.

Unlike her little sister, her swift bare feet molded into the clumps of pasture grass, and she sped along.

Francie grabbed her sister by one wrist and pulled her onward.

The bull was so close that by the time they neared the barbed-wire fence, they could smell the salty sweat on his hide.

She had Little Bea lie down and fold her arm. She rolled her under the fence. Then she did the same.

They stood up.

The bull stopped twenty feet from the post and barbed-wire fence. He stood stomping the ground with his hooves and shaking his long horns menacingly at the sisters. Slobber streamed from his mouth and steam from his nostrils.

She hugged Little Bea protectively. They sat watching the bull from the other side of thin wire as he stared back at them. Francie realized it wasn't Mr. Pratt who was the threat to children that folks warned about. It was the temperamental bull who guarded his domain.

Francie held the same little sister's hand protectively that she had hurt only minutes into their adventure. She loved her sister.

Frightened, Shug stood paralyzed in the middle of the lake waiting for Francie to do something.

She had to think quickly.

"Listen carefully," she said to her little sister. "I think bulls hate the color red. That's why bullfighters use red capes. Take off your red sundress and give it to me."

"No!"

"I said yes. It's an emergency."

"But somebody might see me."

"We've got to save Shug, don't we?"

"Go get Daddy," urged Little Bea. She held tightly to her torn sash.

"Get up and take off your dress," Francie demanded.

"Take off yours, bossy," retorted Little Bea, "He might like your daisy one better."

"I don't have anything on underneath, and you have on a full slip."

She continued, "Bea, we've got to draw the bull's attention so Jordan can run to safety. Anyway, you must mind me. Dad said so before we left."

Under the command of their misguided leader, Little Bea whimpered, stood up, and began to unbutton her red sundress.

Francie led her sister down to the far end of the pasture where the dairy cows were standing, huddled together. She helped her out of her sundress and gave her a boost up into a June apple tree at the fence line. She tied the dress to a long stick and handed the stick up to her sister.

"Wave the dress, Little Bea," Francie instructed. "He'll come down here, and that should give Shug time to make a run for it."

When Little Bea did as she was told, the dress danced a jig, but the bull wasn't interested in it. She tried several more times, then climbed down and went to the fence.

"Here, Mr. Bull, nice old Mr. Bull."

When she dangled the dress over the fence, the curious cows moved in closer, mooing in deep tones. Their cow bells clanked slowly as they ambled in.

The bull, who had not taken his stare off Francie, now watched his herd. After glancing back and forth between Little Bea with the dangling sundress and Francie at some distance, he began moving toward his herd.

Francie motioned all-clear for Shug to come out of the water. He waded to the shore and ran full speed toward her.

When Shug neared the fence, the bull stopped and turned back. A cow bell clanged loudly. It panicked him. He thought it was the bull. He slid into the fence post trying to get under.

Francie pulled him under the bottom wire to safety.

"O-o-o, we-e-e!" he screamed in pain.

"I've got a splinter in my …" Shug stopped short of saying where.

Modestly he tried to cover his front and backsides. Then, indignantly, the nine-year-old huffed, "Let's just go."

When Little Bea ran up to them with the sundress still tied to the stick, Shug grabbed for it.

"Gimme it," he demanded.

"But what will I wear?" asked Little Bea.

Shug untied the dress and slid into it like a housecoat. He swore them to secrecy over this act of humiliation.

Francie walked ahead of them feeling exhilarated. She hadn't been afraid of that silly bull at all! It'd only been a game to her.

Shug yelled out, "You heard me, Francie Kirwin. And I mean it. I really, really mean it. If you tell anyone about this dress, especially Vin', I'll put blood-thirsty ticks in your bed every night for a zillion years!"

Francie walked backwards, facing them. "It's your own fault, runt. I told you not to go swimming."

Shug's face looked raging mad. He wrapped the skirt part of the dress around his injured side as he limped toward home.

Little Bea looked equally embarrassed in her slip.

Shug called out to her. "Hey, Little Bea, who got us into this mess anyway?"

"You did."

"Did not," denied Shug.

Alert for retaliation, he kept paces back from Francie.

"Well, whose idea was it to go through Mr. Pratt's pasture in the first place?

Little Bea answered spontaneously. "Francie's."

"Right, Francie's."

He picked up a rock in his right hand and held the skirt in the other.

"Let's get her!"

Meanwhile, the highway management team in the work trailer had been watching out the window at the three children's antics.

Now that the episode was ending with them running down the side road and out of sight, one warned the others, "Don't go to the end of this road, men, it's not safe. There are dangerous folk who live there. They're as wild as savages."

As the three children got out of sight, the construction team heard a blast that frightened the dairy cows, sending them scattering.

"Was that a shotgun or a car backfiring?" one man asked.

It was Carmen's old van loaded with food donations for the migrant camp workers crashing into a ditch on Plank Road just past the church. A gun blast from a passing truck shot Carmen in the face and left Laurice and Lin splattered with Carmen's brains and banged up in the crash.

Pulling out in front of a vehicle can turn quickly into road rage. But from the Sheer Success Beauty Emporium's parking lot, the truck's young driver had timed his maneuver with precision. So had the experienced shooter. It was not road rage.

CHAPTER 15

Blessed are the Available

Have you noticed that only in times of illness or disaster or death are people real?
—Walter Percy, writer

Carmen Kirwin O'Rourke's funeral became a social event, judging by the number of ladies' hats, high heels, and men in suits in sweltering summer heat. Folks were generous in their expressions of sympathy, filling the sanctuary with cut flower sprays of carnations and roses in pastel colors.

Rory and Laurice were overwhelmed with grieving children for days before the funeral could be held. They held each of the five of them in turn. They soothed them with comforting words. They assured them over and over that they loved them. That's all they knew to do.

In the middle of the night, the couple cried together in bed. They felt blessed for all the sisterly sacrifices Carmen had made for them. They laughed recalling her forgetfulness. They remembered her generosity despite her lack of financial planning.

Nightly Rory dreamed of the siblings' summer childhoods spent swimming and playing. He dreamed of the Christmas morning Carmen had gotten her first show horse, and he had gotten a miniature pony to ride.

Each morning before sunrise, he was awakened from the same nightmare—her driving off in her new Volkswagen van with her new husband for a Woodstock music festival honeymoon with him running behind it shouting out for her to stop.

"Don't go! Don't leave me!" He shouted from his bed, remembering the dream and the loss he had felt when he was a young teenager left alone on a lonely farm.

That her gruesome death made statewide news for days affected absolutely no one at all outside Dixie County.

For those who knew Carmen's community involvement best, gaping questions were raised. Who will provide in-home meals for the homebound elderly? Who will make her delicious squash pickles and coconut cakes? Who will sing high soprano in the church choir? Who will direct Christmas carolers in the nursing home? Who will replace her as cakes and pastries' judge at the county fair? Who will drive me to doctors' appointments? And who will pick me up from the airport?

After the funeral service, close family and friends convened at Merrifield Farm for a meal provided by church ladies in the county. More personal questions were asked. What happens to poor little Jordan? Will Vincent take hardship leave? Do both O'Rourke boys feel like orphans now? Why was it a closed casket funeral? Why was her funeral held inside the church when she was not in good standing? Who shot her and why? Have they found the killer? Can I buy any quilts she has remaining?

The spread of food the church ladies put out on the twenty-four-foot length of folding banquet tables under the big oak tree was as high society as it gets in Dixie County. Lace tablecloths, crocheted tablecloths, tatted tablecloths overlapped end-to-end and hung over the sides like drifts of white and ivory clouds. Two flower vases filled with yellow forsythia, magnolia blooms, white narcissus, and ferns were centerpieces made by Ms. Dovie who knew Carmen loved natural flower arrangements. Circle and oval shapes of each church lady's prized heirloom bone china added elegance and color. Blue Willow by Spode, Old Country Roses by Royal Albert, and several Lenox patterns were represented on serving bowls and platters. To discerning eyes (and there were plenty of them), tucked in-between were regular use plastic Tupperware and Cornflower Blue Corning Ware bowls.

Under the shady oak tree between the house and cottage, the church ladies chatted in hushed tones as they set out platters of ham and fried chicken, bowls of green beans and creamed corn, mashed potatoes with chicken gravy, chilled sliced tomatoes and cucumbers, and deep-dish peach cobblers and fried apple pies. More food kept arriving with guests until the tables were full.

Men waited at the periphery for the blessing.

Rory choked out a few kind words, thanking everyone for being there to honor Carmen.

Vincent tried to speak but couldn't. Several men patted the two on their backs.

Rory asked Pastor Pate to say grace, and he did. A long one.

Then Vincent joined his cousins and friends up in the climbing tree away from the numbing questions. He and Francie held Jordan between them on a large horizontal branch. Nearby, Kimberlee and Lin sat close to Beatrice. Solemn faced, they watched the mourners. Their own innocence was gone with the lingering image of Carmen's gruesome wounds stamped on their minds.

Without her laughter, they had no reason to laugh.

Without her free spirit, they had no reason to fly.

Albert had been traumatized watching his aunt's casket lowered into the ground and then covered with a heavy pile of dirt. He would not leave his mother's arms and had not spoken since the burial service. The five-year-old reverted to sucking his thumb.

After the burial Everett had stopped by to check on Mrs. Ludeke and Bonita and to finish packing his gear. He was heading out early in the morning. He was mildly surprised that his fiancée, Lin, had accepted a permanent job caregiving for Mrs. Ludeke. It was part time until Bonita's family moved on to their next harvest.

As he was going to his rental car, he noticed a shadowy figure skulking in the tall privet bushes at the property line.

"Hey, you," he called out, nonplussed.

"Huh?"

"What are you doing, pervert? Spying on grieving people?" Everett asked in a strong voice. Then, "Hey, I know you. From the church steps."

Wyatt moved toward him, "Yep. So what, boy?"

"Stop there. You're not welcome here, *boy.*"

"I know'd that. Just came to pay my respects. I usted be friends of theirs," explained Wyatt walking away, both hands shoved into his jeans pockets.

"Keep going. Don't cause these good folks any problems today."

Everett got in his car and watched the skulking man walk down the driveway slowly.

Although he had bundles of money, Wyatt Hugg knew he was uneducated and outclassed. Crass even. He was never able to figure out why the Kirwin family had suddenly cut off all association with him. Jokes are jokes. And it had been a funny joke he'd played on Ms. Anne Bea right before she died. No harm, no foul, right?

He and Rory had been sitting on the tailgate of his truck drinking a few canned brews at Rory's mailbox on April 15, the start of planting season according to the

Farmers' Almanac. Ahead of them, Ms. Anne Bea and the oldest little girl were in her garden planting tomato plants she had started in her kitchen window from seeds.

She was down on her knees digging holes and loosening the plowed dirt before the oldest little girl would stick a small green plant into the hole up to the first stem. The old woman would cover it with the loose soil then tamp it into place, being careful not to disturb the few that had blooms. She could do two or three holes before needing to get up and move down the row. Wyatt had noted how bent the old woman's back was both kneeling and standing. He had wondered if the cancer had done that to her.

It was seven thirty when the last tomato plant was set. When the old woman and the oldest little girl were walking home with their tools and empty starter pots, he casually called out to them, "Weatherman sezs it's gonna frost to-night. All dem 'mater plants gonna turn to sl-i-me when they fre-e-ze."

It was funny. He had just made it up on the spur of the moment to get a rise from his former schoolteacher. And maybe he had said it to pay her back for the times she had sent him to the principal's office. He would have told her it was a joke, but she had chimed in and told him to "go read a book." He'd hated it when he was in school and teachers said that to him.

He'd learned later that Ms. Anne Bea went home, ate a sorghum biscuit, and drank a glass of buttermilk for a late supper. She returned to her garden where she gently troweled up each tomato plant so as not to damage its fragile roots. She arranged it carefully in a straw market basket lined with damp newspaper. By herself she'd managed to get five baskets of tomato plants back to her house where she set them in a neat row on the dining room table like a newborn nursery scene of premature green babies.

She went to bed and died in her sleep that night.

"Not my fault," Wyatt continued to tell himself, remembering how Rory had bloodied his nose at his mother's funeral.

That's why he knew not to show up at Carmen's funeral. He'd had a fifteen-year-long fascination with her. She had long blonde hair and frequent singing gigs on local television shows. She was the closest thing to a beautiful movie star he'd ever gotten close to. Really close to. His infatuation with her grew into a one-way fantasized relationship to the point of what some folks would call stalking her.

Is watching someone through their window stalking? No. Is sitting in her van stalking? No. Is watching her swim nude in her creek stalking? No, according to Wyatt, he was protecting her and staking his claim on her.

About ten years ago when Edna Mae was pregnant, he decided to let Carmen know how much in love he was with her. One night about midnight when she went out to her van to load boxes of Ball canning jars, he jumped out of the van to tell her. When he saw that she was in a thin nightgown and that he could make out her curvy silhouette, he skipped words of love and pinned her to the floorboard and raped her. She fought back. There may have been some brutality involved; he couldn't remember.

He knew the little boy was his. She'd known it but kept silent. Didn't he owe her the respect of getting to go to her funeral? He'd killed the two pieces of trash for her. He'd turned all his rage and frustration to the subhumans Carmen had chosen over him.

Everett honked his car horn lightly at the Ludekes' mailbox.

"Get on down the road. I'm watching you."

Wyatt pouted as he shuffled down Kirwin Lane toward Plank Road. The predator was watching someone else, too. That oldest little girl first. Later, the other one.

They sure were pretty.

CHAPTER 16

The Memory Keepers' Boxes

The function of education is to teach one to think intensively and to think critically. Intelligence plus character—that is the goal of true education.

—MARTIN LUTHER KING, JR.

When Laurice stepped into the spring house to see the open chest and the clothesline strung with a colorful canopy of others' accomplishments, an epiphany hit her, that one day her oldest daughter would write about the family that adopted her.

Public schools in Dixie County started back in session in mid-August. Francie and Kimberlee vowed to put off clearly stupid freshman markers such as holding hands with each other, swapping clothes and makeup, and falling *up* the interior stairwell in the main building. They were sophomores now. Much had changed over the summer.

For one, Kimberlee talked constantly about Vincent now. She did not linger at her locker or the water fountain to talk to high school boys. She watched the classroom clock anticipating three o'clock when Vincent would pick her up at school. She skipped several majorette practices with the band to spend afternoons at the lake or walking downtown Ellisville together. He would drop her off at her house before dark so she would have enough time to do homework.

The second change was harder for others to detect, but Francie's mother had seen it. She recognized the signs of depression that Francie exhibited daily. Her dark moods, lethargy, and disinterest in participating in family times were signals something was bothering her.

Laurice asked Francie if she wanted to talk.

"No. I'm fine," Francie answered, waking from a school day nap.

"No. You're not. Are you still thinking about Auntie Carmen a lot?"

"Well, not so much. I still don't want to forget her, ever."

"You won't. We won't," said Laurice.

Francie asked her mother if the elbow group member, Bobo-something, who said shooting Carmen was accidental had his court trial yet. The driver was charged also.

"That's next week."

"Can I go?"

"No. Not unless they call you to testify."

"I see. Still too young. Still too dumb. Just a nothing," Francie snapped.

"Honey, what are you talking about? Help me understand."

Francie sat up in her bed, surrounded by her homework and textbooks. They scattered.

"I don't like my new classrooms, Mama. They're in Building 3 where the upper classmen are. I'm a nobody this year, just like last. It was supposed to be different.

"My teachers are so very hard. In my advanced classes, there is a ton of homework to do each night. I can't watch the little ones and get through all of it. I'm so tired.

"I need the evening newspaper every day now. That's just for an elective. I told Dad but he forgets to buy me one. I must write a summary with facts on one news story every night. Can't fake it," she said, throwing back the light covers.

She continued with her next reason.

"Kimberlee's not in my study hall this year. I sit along the back wall of the juniors' chemistry class with four other sophomores. I feel like such a baby there."

She sat up, dangling her legs off the side of the bed.

"Glenn's still bringing me home. That's the only bright spot in my day. When I get home, Beatrice must read aloud to me. Bert just wants me to hold him while he sucks his thumb."

"I see," said Laurice, patting her leg. "School, babysitting, and homework are too much for you right now."

Francie burst into tears. "I can't do it."

Her mother let her cry a few moments. *It's cathartic*, she thought.

Then she said to her teenager, "Lin and I were talking about this very thing yesterday," said Laurice with a smile. "She's offered to babysit the little ones in the afternoons so you could get your studies done."

"She did?"

"She did. Your dad agrees with me that you need your own quiet place to study and to be with your own thoughts. We're going to empty out the springhouse and set you up a study area there. You won't be disturbed."

"Y'all would do that for me?" asked Francie, wiping the corners of her eyes with a tissue.

"Yes. You'd be close enough to help Lin if the boys got too rowdy."

"When?"

"Maybe Saturday."

"I would love that, Mama."

Laurice hugged her daughter, thinking poignantly how fast the next three years would pass.

"Just remember, Francie, you're not moving into a college dorm in another state. I want to see you every evening to chat a while."

"Sure, Mama."

"You meet or exceed all your academic class assignments, and the deal holds. Otherwise, it becomes *my* respite room!"

The excitement of having a place of her own was akin to getting her driving permit to Francie.

On Saturday, she arose at dawn and ran down to the springhouse with cleaning supplies. She picked up everything she could identify as junk. Overhead was a maze of clotheslines that zigzagged back and forth across the entire length and width of the springhouse to dry clothes like rugs, rags, and sheets. She pulled items off and piled them in the galvanized tub that had been used for baths before indoor plumbing.

On a dusty easel was a canvas where her dad was painting a picture of Noccalula Falls from a magazine picture he had taped to the easel. He'd been working on it for years at "glacial speed," he'd teased. She moved it to a corner and packed away his paints and brushes.

She cleaned the windows with vinegar and rags.

Inside on the uphill side of the springhouse, earthen shelves had been dug into the dirt staggered up about halfway. Then the framed wall started. The shelves were filled with jars of canned peaches, pickles, tomatoes, relishes, and peas. The cool niche created a mural of colorful glass, so Francie left them as they were.

She washed some empty jars in a pan, filling it from the tapped spring inside. She set them along the windowsills along the long wall. Clear, green, amber, and purple ones made a colorful and inexpensive display.

She swept the dirt floor. Its surface was as hard packed as baked clay pottery. She spread out the rag rug she'd helped Auntie Carmen make from scrap sewing material.

The screen door needed repairing and its rusty springs replaced. Each time it was opened, it squealed a discordant note, and the flies invited themselves inside.

"Welcome!" she said with a grand gesture when Vincent and Rory entered with a large industrial desk. It took up half the room. She had the men move out the galvanized bathtub. This created just the right amount of space for the desk and a chair.

After lunch, Francie returned with her books and desk supplies. She was settled in before Kimberlee drove up in her mother's truck.

"Hey, hon,' I wanted to s-e-e whut you're do-i-n-g. Vin-c-e-n, bless his little pea-picking heart, told me abo-u-t it. I miss seein' ya at school, ya know," said Kimberlee, bouncing in with her baton. She twirled it horizontally, passing it from hand to hand.

She continued, "I saw you and Glenn at sch-o-o-l. O-h-h, my gosh! He's so hot! If I wernt so-o-o set on mar-r-i-n' Vin'c-e-n-, I'd go after him-m-ah. His family has *mon-ey*, ya know."

"I'm not 'going after him,' Kimberlee," Francie corrected. "I have study hall in his chemistry class due to overcrowding. He walks me to my next classroom."

"*Tisk, tisk.* It's a shame that he's yur second cousin and a-l-l that," Kimberlee said.

"Third. By marriage," Francie corrected.

"Does by marriage still count as in-ce-est?" Kimberlee asked.

"No. Auntie Carmen said we were third cousins, same as Queen Elizabeth and Prince Philip of England," Francie answered what she recognized as an intentional jab.

She was beginning to not like Kimberlee so much. She shot back, "He's really smart. He's going to become an astronaut."

Kimberlee faked a yawn. She sat in the desk chair.

"That'll nev-ah happen. No-bod-e-e from Dixie County has ev-ah done anythin' important lik that. I, on the other hand, wi-l-ll be crowned Miss Al-ah-bam-er one day, maybe even Miss 'Merica, en then I'll marry Vin-c-e-n and live here beside Ma and Pa."

Vincent heard his name as he pushed through the screen door. It squealed its awful sound, and the tension spring slammed it shut with a bang.

He held a stack of what looked like luggage. He had a rolled-up rug over his shoulder.

Arlo followed close at his heels.

"Hello, girls," Vincent said, smiling.

"Well, if'n ya don't lo-o-ok lik a peddler with wares to s-e-l-l. Whut 'cha selling, sold-i-e-r?" commented Kimberlee, flirting.

She sashayed over to help him. She wore cheek-revealing Daisy Duke cutoff shorts and a school athletic tank top. She struck a pose, propping on her baton.

She gave him a knowing wink, "I'm here to see Fran-ci-ee's study stud-i-o. A'wella now, I've see-en it, and I'm red-de-e to find some fun. Wanta co-m-e with me, big fella?"

He eyed Kimberlee's pose. "Yea, Kim, I do. Let's go."

He set the big pieces down. The smaller boxes he set on top of the desk.

He explained to Francie, "I'm clearing out the cottage. Not very manly for me and Jordan. The big one, the trunk, is full of Mother and Granny Bea's keepsakes. I thought you should have them. I don't know what's in those pretty boxes there. Mother kept them on top of the chifforobe for years. Anyway … uh-h-h, they're yours, if you want them. This is a good place. Lots of high storage up there."

He pointed to a small open loft area where a family of barn owls lived their reclusive lives in a dark corner.

"Down here's better," said Francie. "And what's that?"

Vincent unrolled the heavy tapestry—a scene with Turkish belly dancers in skimpy costumes. He explained the wall hanging was a gift from a foreign missionary the Kirwins had sponsored in the past.

Rolled out on top of the rag rug, the exotic rug looked vulgar and hideous to them. The teenage girls tried belly dancing with Mason jar bands as finger cymbals. Vincent sprawled on top of the tapestry, grabbing at the teens' legs as they danced around him in a circle until Kimberlee fell into his lap.

They were laughing when they heard "hello" from outside.

They froze in their silliness.

"Yes?" said Francie, straightening up. She recognized Glenn walking up to the screen door. "Glenn!"

"Yep. Thought I'd come see if I could help y'all fix up the study room," he said.

"It's turning into a clubhouse," said Vincent, good-naturedly. He got up and shook Glenn's hand. "Been a long time, my man."

"You bet. How's it going?"

"Fine. We were just leaving, Kim and me. Gonna go now and let y'all visit."

Glenn stepped aside in the small space so the couple could exit.

"Bye, hon'ee, luv ya," Kimberlee called out, proudly wrapped arm-in-arm with Vincent, not realizing she'd left her baton behind.

Francie became self-conscious as Glenn looked around. She was certain he'd never seen a room with a dirt floor before. Yet, it seemed to hold his interest.

Pointing along the jars on the dirt shelves, he jested. "Food for thought, I see."

"Every student needs some," she replied, smiling at his sense of humor. She added, "I like to dig in."

"Yep, I get it, Francie. Funny," he replied smiling.

After a glance down at the tapestry, he gestured, "And I supposed this is the layout for your new Turkish bath?"

"Is that where they are? We thought it was a palace," Francie commented. "This used to be a bathhouse before indoor plumbing with the spring tapped here."

"I saw the tub outside," he said.

He picked up the baton. "And this, a modern bath accessory?"

"Yep. Backscratcher for sensitive skin. Two sizes."

He looked up into the rafters at the moon pie faces of three owls, their heads tilted at the same angle, and said, "And wisdom from above, too."

"Yep, the three wise men. They teach me history."

"Why's that?" he smiled. His dark eyes were keen on her face.

He took a step toward her.

"They're always asking me 'who.'"

"Who wrote the US Constitution?" he queried.

"James Madison."

Glenn took another step closer to her.

"Who likes you?"

"Who? Who? Who?" Francie asked, coyly.

"I do."

Francie tried to act indifferent. "I thought you were just the boy who, get it 'who,' gives me transportation home from school."

He repeated himself, tilting his head in the owls' whimsical way, "I am. Do you have a boyfriend?"

"No. At the moment, I'm available," she answered, blushing.

"Let me be your boyfriend—official boyfriend. The kind the whole school knows about."

He stood as close to her as possible without coming into contact.

Francie turned and looked up at the owls. She pretended to be having a conversation with them. She turned back to Glenn.

"They advise *yes*, you may," she answered. She had liked him for four months but had admitted it to no one. His direct style was new and charming to her.

"Then I think I'm going to kiss you. Right now. Like immediately," he said, pulling her close and kissing her lightly on the lips. *First kiss lightly and gentlemanly,* he'd read.

"But we're cousins."

"Not really."

"Third cousins, my aunt said."

"Not really."

"No?"

"No."

"Well, then kiss me again."

After kissing her longer and with more feeling, he held her close. She felt stiff. He bent to nuzzle her neck. She pulled away slightly.

He stopped making advances, proud of his self-control but needing a quick diversion.

He stepped nonchalantly to the desk and asked about the decorative boxes on it. Francie explained that they were writings her grandmother had done over the years.

"Like journaling? he asked, sitting in the office chair. "Well, read me something," he said, pulling her down onto his lap.

Her heart was racing, but she was trying to appear cool. She opened the top box decorated with roses. She took out a school spiral notebook and opened it randomly. She put on her new glasses and began to read aloud:

August 30, 1965

Clyde thought it best to drive me to school today instead of me waiting on the bus at our mailbox. He wanted me to get to my classroom early and be settled in safely before school opens. I can imagine he's sitting in his truck in the parking lot in a spot that offers the widest, best view of events that might unfold for better or worse. I am grateful every day for his love and protection.

As I write this at seven o'clock, many schools will be opening their doors soon for the school year 1965–66. In Dixie County, integration of schools may get many parents interested in their children's education for the first time in the life of the rural family. I pray that be so as Americans are guaranteed free public education through twelfth grade. How much of a stretch is it to not segregate students by color? Negro boys and girls attend with white students in other parts of America. Why not here?

The point I am trying to capture for posterity is my hope that school integration works, not just today but down that long road ahead. In an academic setting, teachers practice neutrality every day. All students are given attention. Some more at one time, less at another. Our expectations for each student may be different because we push them to reach his or her potential. We can help any student with a teachable spirit, if parents will back us with discipline at home and if principals will keep their eyes on the big picture—graduating educated students ready for the workforce.

Today's civics' lesson is the meaning of community.

—A. B.

"That's cool," said Glenn. "You should keep that."

"I am. I'm now the official keeper of the memory boxes," Francie affirmed proudly.

Glenn asked for another excerpt. Francie closed that notebook and opened another, an old black and white composition book. Again, she randomly turned to an entry. It was handwritten and dated March 1930.

One thing I've become convinced of since moving to Littafuchee is how much genetics rules our lives. Take Clyde's family. They're so musically talented they don't even need to rehearse. I can't sing or play an instrument, yet he and his sisters can play all of them! Why would he want to marry such an odd, untalented bird as I am?

Regarding genetics and shades of auburn hair. There are hundreds everywhere you go in Dixie County. It's like everybody's using from the same shampoo bottle some trickster replaced with red hair dye.

I wonder who the patriarch of this trait was and how long ago it was? Had to be after 1819 when Alabama became a state and settlers started moving in through the northern routes. Perhaps there was a large clan originally from Scotland or Ireland. Most have big brown eyes and freckles. I love freckles! Sunshine kisses.

Poor posture. I think that's not genetic but learned. Everybody here has such poor posture. Look up! There's so much to see. I will. I declare here and now that I will correct this habit in my students!

In one poor family, the Tommsons, the entire clan of forty folks looks identical. They are all extremely light complected and wear permanently lethargic expressions, as if they've never experienced excitement in their entire lives. In addition to poor posture, they are extremely shy and cautious of outsiders. I've been told they've intermarried, only sporadically marrying mates from outside the clan.

They have a tendency toward frequently broken bones. This gene is showing up earlier and earlier in their offspring. I've identified one boy with good potential, a student of mine. He's got a bright mind, but his gait is very unsteady. He's had a broken wrist and broken tibia from falls this school year. I hope and pray he makes it to adulthood. I do not suspect physical abuse. I did a home visit. They gave me a goat!

The Tommsons are indifferent to the world outside Littafuchee valley. They accept everything that happens to them and ask no one for favors. They just splint their own limbs and continue about their business, which is doing nothing, as best as I can determine. None have the strength to farm their hundred acres of prime real estate beside the railroad tracks. It has remained uncultivated for as long as Clyde can remember.

This week I asked my student's mother if I could take the boy to the Jefferson-Hillman Hospital as a charity patient for a proper diagnosis. Afraid of doctors and welfare workers and the government, she declined. She sent a chipped milk churn to my house today to thank me for my concern.

Sometimes it's as if I've moved to a third world country.

—A.B.

Francie closed the notebook. "It's so sad."

"Not at all," replied Glenn.

He had both arms around her middle so she couldn't get up.

He explained, "Think about how far our school system has come since your grandmother was a newlywed teaching here. Think about high school. It's tough. That's good. Graduates can get accepted into any university. And where are the Tommsons? Gone. That clan vanished. Not our concern anymore."

"You're right," said Francie. She thought to herself that the school year was looking better. *I'll have to tell Mama about him.*

On Sunday, Glenn sat with her at church. The two of them drove to the new McDonald's in the next county for lunch. On Monday, he drove Francie home from school again and asked to hear some more of her grandmother's old journal entries.

They parked. He got some of his last year's notebooks out of his trunk. They walked down the path filled with old growth dogwoods, azaleas, and magnolias. She told him that all the flowers and planting areas on the old side where they were had been Granny Bea's projects. She loved to paint the hillside with flowers. She explained that her aunt took care of the flower gardens after Granny Bea died.

"When was that?" he asked.

"Three years ago."

"Two family members in three years. That's tough," he said. "You're resilient."

"Maybe I am."

"So, you had lots of springs and summers to learn gardening from them both?"

he asked, then stated, "I like daffodils and azaleas in the spring. We have those at our house."

She forewarned him that she had lots of homework to do and that there were other things of Granny Bea and Auntie Carmen's she hadn't looked at yet. Did he want to look at those quickly before her mother got home?

"Sure," was his reply.

Inside the springhouse, they moved the trunk onto the Turkish tapestry and sat down. Francie opened it to find placed carefully on top her grandfather's military uniform with bars and pins on his jacket. He had served in World War 1 in the Army Signal Corps. She found a small stack of old, yellowed letters pinned with a rusted safety pin inside the jacket. The letters were to Dilly Gillivray. Was their placement symbolic? Francie found it difficult to read his handwriting. Much of it was blacked out.

"You read this one to me," Francie said, handing an opened letter to Glenn.

He began. The salutation was to "My Sweet Potato."

They laughed.

> We await orders. It is cold and wet outside, but we manage okay in our tents. Boredom is a nasty varmint that robs us of our will to do anything at all. Homesickness is rampant among the troops. It has no cure but home where I can be with you, my doting sisters Agnes and Estes, and eating a fine Sunday dinner they'll prepare. Afterward we would (blacked out) and I would sleep for twelve hours in my own bed. Cold and hungry I wait in formation to (blacked out) which will determine (blacked out) Will you wait for me if I (blacked out).

"Nope, Sweet Potato didn't wait," Francie said. She folded the letter and pinned it back with the others. Perhaps she would read more later. "Yep, my Granny Bea was jealous."

Digging down, they found blue baby booties from the baby who died, blue and red school ribbons, awards, and recognitions for civic work for Anne Bea and Clyde and for their children, Carmen and Rory.

There was a small photo album disintegrating from age. Inside printed in her hand were names and dates of pictures of her birth family. Francie especially liked the one of her with all her many nieces and nephews outside the steps of their home in Montgomery. She could make out the capitol building in the distance. Wearing a fur coat, Anne Bea was holding Christmas presents wrapped in plain parcel paper and string. At her feet was a sack of oranges and a long stem of bananas the way they grow on trees. There was an even older lithograph of her parents sitting in a parlor. She was wearing a stylish dark bonnet and long dress and holding a toddler who was frowning. The father was holding a newborn on a white pillow. The baby, in a lacy christening gown, was Anne Beatrice.

Francie closed the photo album. There would be time to look through it more carefully later.

On the bottom packed flat were poster projects her students had made. Francie took them out in one batch.

"Let's put them up," said Glenn. He took one and stapled it to the wall. It was a map showing the sixty-seven counties in the state of Alabama.

"Looks good," said Francie. "Let's hang a few more."

Glenn hung a heavy display of Native American arrowheads and broken points with the title, "Found in Dixie County," and another project showing the different tribes in Alabama. He picked out a picture and student's report on Wernher von Braun at Redstone Arsenal.

Francie propped a poster board on the art easel. She read off the names of the major rivers in the state: Tennessee, Mississippi, Black Warrior, Locust Fork, Mulberry Fork, Cahaba, Alabama, Tombigbee, Sipsey, Coosa, Tallapoosa, Conecuh, Pea, Choctawhatchee, and Chattahoochee. She noted a sidebar that held the fact that the Five Rivers area of the Mobile Bay included the Mobile, Spanish, Tensaw, Apalachee, and Blakeley Rivers.

They moved on to the box of prize ribbons and hung them on the clothesline.

They were just about to take a break when Rory walked over from across the highway via the concrete culvert. He had seen a strange car parked close to the springhouse and went to investigate.

"Yoo-hoo, anybody studying?" he called.

"Hey, dad, come on in. Glenn's been helping me go through Granny Bea's things. When we're through, he's going to help me with geometry, right Glenn?"

Glenn put out his hand and shook Rory's. "I brought some of my old workbooks from Mrs. Nelson's class."

"Mrs. Nelson? I had her too," said Rory.

Francie told her father that Glenn planned to become an astronaut.

"Actually, an aeronautical engineer, sir," Glenn clarified.

"You don't say," said Rory, who held the local opinion of anyone from Littafuchee's slim chance to achieve a major level of success. No one famous or important had been born in Littafuchee. No actor. No Olympian. No astronaut. No elected official. No writer. No Miss Alabama. No university football player.

"Good luck, son," he said before leaving. "Don't make things too easy for her, Glenn. She's got to get the math and science down for herself."

"Right, sir."

When Rory left, they took two bottles of soda from the frigid spring water, two boxes of keepsakes off the desk, and went out to sit on the creek bank.

"Read to me," Glenn asked.

He removed his shoes and put his feet into the water. Then he took off Francie's tennis shoes and socks. He kissed one ankle and placed that foot into the water. The second foot, too.

Everything he does seems so natural, she thought. *What can I do that girlfriends do?*

Francie opened one box and flipped through the contents. "These are old. They are my grandmother's short stories she wrote about an Indian princess named Half-Moon. I'll save them for later. Maybe Beatrice should hear them, too.

"What's in the other one?"

"Well, let's find out," Francie said.

She pulled her feet out of the water and draped them across his lap. He smiled and inched closer to her. She was proud of herself for thinking about doing that.

Francie opened the second box to find loose pages of all sizes and dates. Some were typed and some handwritten. She pulled out a typewritten one as it was easier to read.

> June 1935
> Sunday afternoon I watched two hundred Protestants from five surrounding counties receive baptism in the Locust Fork River. It ended a ten-day tent revival held at the agricultural fairgrounds. It was interdenominational and featured evangelists from three denominations.
>
> The Birmingham newspapers proclaimed it the beginning of a new spiritual movement. It came as welcome relief from the despair

experienced by farmers who have not been getting good value for their crops. We know. Clyde has had to dip into his savings a little each year until there is nothing in our nest egg. As spendthrift as they are, Miss Agnes and Miss Estes' inheritances have dropped as they begin to underwrite Merrifield Farm's expenses. I do not receive my trust money until 1943.

As it appears to me, the bulk of the two hundred folks fall into two categories. Those hedging their bets with God through rebaptism and young children about five to ten-years-old who have been frightened throughout the revival by loud, pounding, prancing, perspiring evangelists who yelled at them that the devil will steal their souls and that they might die tomorrow unsaved and go to hell. I doubt the truth of these statements. God bless them. As soon as I can, I will talk one-on-one with the children from our church about my faith in a loving Lord who does not want to punish me but to walk beside me through life as my loving heavenly Father.

Clyde's gospel quartet sang each night of the revival with a line-up of talent fit for The Grand Old Opry in Nashville. I ride up with him each day after school. I am bone-weary tired of these late nights. After the first hour when his group sings, I go to the truck to grade school papers. I know what goes on up in these remote hills. I have stayed alert, ready to hit reverse gear and exit fast if I see them start bringing out snakes at these meetings.

There was silence.

"The end," said Francie.

"Wow!" said Glenn. "You can't make that stuff up."

They sat silent for several more moments.

When Francie got up, the box with the earlier stories fell open and out rolled a royal blue satin pouch. Inside was a pink arrowhead which Glenn said was made of rose quartz. She thought it was lovely and held it to her heart.

"I'm sure there's a story behind this pink arrowhead in this memory box," Francie said to Glenn. "I'm going to keep it out. Put it in my jewelry box at home."

"Well, if you're going to do that, let me make a necklace out of it," said Glenn. "I've got some leather strap at home. I'll bind it well for you."

He slid it into his jeans pocket without asking. The new memory keeper felt extremely uncomfortable about that. And the fact that he had never once noticed her new eyeglasses.

CHAPTER 17

Armed and Angry Keepers of the Soil

It was times like this when I thought my father, who hated guns and had never been to any wars, was the bravest man who ever lived.

—Harper Lee

Rory Kirwin grew nervous about having the incorporation meeting at Merrifield Farm. The late afternoon temperature registered 102 degrees, exceeding the limit for cool, rational discussions among men with differing opinions.

The cloudburst that fell minutes earlier had Merrifield Farm in a surreal mist of gray steam that arose from the hot soil in curling drifts from the grass, the driveway, the garden, and between buildings. The released steam was pulled by the mild breeze across the homestead up into the cliffs and treetops of Arrowhead Mountain.

Rory's starched white, button-down church shirt clung to his chest, damp with perspiration and as limp as today's wet wash. Streams of sweat trickled down his back in rivulets that merged, angling toward the center of his buttocks where his long blue jeans and his leather boots trapped the back sweat and body heat against his skin.

Is it the heat or a case of nerves? It is as hot as the hinges to hell today, he thought to himself.

It would have been the end of a regular workday. Food, then rest. Except he wanted this meeting to happen without delay now that barricades and equipment had all been removed, and the final stretch of highway had opened to through traffic. The wide areas on either side of the four-lane were perfect for commercial development.

Whether or not anyone wanted it, fast-food franchises and car dealerships were coming. He wanted to preserve the farmsteads and natural settings as much as possible and saw incorporation as the answer. Planned growth. He knew many folks who agreed.

Rory mopped his face with his blue bordered cotton handkerchief. *Sure hope I'm not stepping into cow manure.*

At any moment Alton Bell, the county extension agent, would arrive with tonight's invited guest, Princeton Brooks, a volunteer businessman who worked with city planners with the Birmingham Regional Planning Commission. Brooks was a friend of the agent, and Bell was a familiar face in Littafuchee.

Bell's job was to help farmers with many of their husbandry problems, such as livestock health issues, how to increase crop yields, and how to manage water runoff and pests. He served as Dixie County's primary liaison with the State Agriculture folks in Auburn.

He'd recently introduced healthier feed blends for cattle. In October, he would judge the students' 4-H projects at the Dixie County Fair.

Rory knew Bell would be the familiar connection between the rural farmers of Littafuchee and the big bank vice president who was going to tell the farmers why they needed to incorporate and how to go about it.

He was determined not to have a repeat of the fiasco from last week when they had met at Harvest Church. The elbow boys and Wyatt Hugg had come to blows over the ballfield relocation. Buster, who painted Confederate flags on barns for a modest living, broke his right wrist in the pile-on started by belligerent Wyatt. A sheriff's deputy was summoned. He ordered Wyatt to stay out of the matter as he was part of the river community, not Littafuchee.

Wyatt swore to get a vote somehow.

Harvest Church banned community meetings.

Rory kept sweeping the yard broom across the shallow pools of rainwater in the ancient, pitted concrete sidewalk off his sister's cottage where masses of black ants had been swept from the grass and underneath the concrete during the cloudburst.

He dreaded the embarrassment of ants crawling onto guests as they entered or marching in through the old cottage's many cracks during the meeting.

Fleetingly he remembered Carmen's rhythmic motions as she had swept the warped porch boards and the pitted walkway of drowned ants after big rains.

Do they drown or crowd together in a desperate attempt to survive? he thought. *I'll ask Sis.*

Remembering Carmen came unexpectedly and always hurt. He could not allow himself to acknowledge the void he felt after her death. He could not admit to his wife the intense pain in his gut that awoke him during the night and lingered throughout the day.

He could not complain. He was a farmer and the patriarch of the family. His duty was to be strong for all those in the family who were doing their own mourning for the beloved soul, the sister who had been the heart and hearth of Merrifield Farm after their own mother's passing.

His attempts to get Littafuchee formally recognized would honor those two respected women.

Extension Agent Bell's familiar Chevy truck shifted into second gear as it headed up the gravel driveway from Kerwin Lane. Rory stepped over to greet the guests, hesitating before leaning the straw broom against a longleaf pine tree trunk.

"Howdy."

"Same at ya."

"Things going well?"

"You betcha."

"Rory, this is Princeton Brooks. He's very active with the BRPC."

Rory extended his hand to the professionally dressed man. Brooks shook it hardily.

Rory said, "Thanks for coming tonight. Hope you can help us. You'll be speaking to an ornery and prideful group of old fellas at this meeting."

"I understand."

"But we must change. Bell told you about my sister, didn't he? What happened to her?"

"Yes, my sympathies to you and your family. And he told me about someone shooting cattle in a field near here."

"Pratt Peterson's."

Brooks said, "You're right. Things like that shouldn't be going on here. This is 1985."

"Yep."

"Yep," echoed Bell.

"Now that the highway's opened through here, things will change. What is to come is not staying what was," said Brooks.

"I think so, too, sir," said Rory. "Any change means letting different people in."

"Integration?" summarized Brooks. "Well, that's been a law since 1954. Don't know how Littafuchee's stayed white this long."

He continued. "I think for the meeting we need to focus on what these other landowners will be gaining. They might just listen."

Rory shook his head *yes.* "It's your show tonight, Mr. Brooks."

He gestured toward the cottage, just steps away.

"I thought we'd meet in my sister's cottage, as it's one of the last original log cabins in these mountains. It was built by my great-great-grandfather about 1840."

Brooks shook his head no. "What about your house? Any problem meeting there?"

"No, but all the kids are there. Kinda noisy."

Brooks smiled and said, "That's fine. It's better, in fact. That points toward where we're headed, not where we've been."

"Yes, sir, Mr. Brooks. It's your show tonight."

Laurice, Vincent, and Francie quickly picked up toys, shoes, and books. The three youngest children were ushered onto the back porch. Laurice excused herself when the first of the neighbors arrived on the doorstep. Vincent took a seat in the living room. He felt out-of-place since he would not be living in Littafuchee.

Rory, Agent Bell, and Mr. Brooks stood at the top of the stairs on the front porch and shook hands with each person as he arrived.

Paul, in his seventies and with a thick head of hair, was in his overalls and waders. He made apologies for his appearance. He entered the house in his sock feet.

John, another seventy-something, removed his cowboy hat politely, nodding but saying nothing.

Colt, the youngest of the first arrivals was sixtyish. He bolted up the steps fit and hearty, saying "howdy" to each person on the porch and shaking hands with the others sitting in a circle of chairs in the living room.

Right on time, 7:30 p.m., several mud-splattered trucks with mud-crusted wheels pulled up the driveway. They parked.

Winston seemed to wear a miffed expression. He had his son, Hunter, fifteen years old, with him. Although they were distant cousins, Rory knew Winston opposed increasing government interference in his business and was probably there to represent the opposition. He owned a small motor repair shop. Hunter had already dropped out of high school to help his dad.

Elderly Samuel Waites wore a portable oxygen tank and was aided by his son, Elvis, who was in his fifties and used a walking cane.

Rory stepped down and walked leisurely over to greet these arrivals.

"Winston, Sam, Hunter, Elvis, I'm glad you came tonight," said Rory. He put his hand on Hunter's shoulder. "Good to see you, young'un, it's been a while."

"Yes sir," replied the handsome lad.

"Yep," said Winston. "Joe said we'd better come, me and Sam. We have something to say."

"I'll bet you do," replied Rory. "You'll get to. And I hope you'll be willing to hear what others have to contribute."

"Well," said Elvis, poking holes in the wet dirt with his walking cane, "Like Winston said, Joe Gillery said we'd better come."

Rory assured them that nothing was to be decided tonight, that Agent Bell had a friend who knew a little bit about helping small communities.

Pete Peterson and Ben Ludeke arrived together, walking the fence line along Kirwin Lane together. They were in deep conversation.

Others arrived, about two dozen total. The youngest was thirty-five-years-old. He represented his great-grandmother, who was frail and mostly bedridden. His name was Jaime Tommson. He was not married or employed. Neither did he have power of attorney for his great-grandmother and her one hundred acres of prime land homesteaded and property tax free as long as she lived.

Rory waved at the wives sitting in trucks and went inside.

After all introductions were made, Rory started the meeting with a quick prayer.

He turned to Agent Bell to introduce the speaker.

Princeton Brooks had assessed his small audience as each arrived. The dissenters and naysayers. The enthusiastic and motivated. The talkers. The listeners. The volunteers.

He knew all had more traits alike than different. They were fiercely independent keepers of the soil who cared not whom they pleased or displeased. They were the current generation of generations of landowners past who lived subsistent lifestyles and had little use for higher education or politics or affluent men who wore their fancy titles like bronze affiliation pins.

Brooks stood at the center of the circle of men. "Gentlemen, may I remove my coat and tie? How did they do summers in the South before air-conditioning?"

"Sure, take it off."

"So that's what they call that tight thing around your neck."

"I thought it was called marriage."

Everyone laughed, and the ice was broken.

Next Brooks would reel them in with a personal anecdote.

"Well, thank you for inviting me, Agent Bell. He told me about some of the happenings here in Littafuchee while we were picking blueberries over at Varina's place."

Someone chimed, "Varina's U-Pick-It?"

"Yes. I was there with my wife and children. We want our kids to know the value of an hour's work, which last weekend just happened to be less than five dollars with a family of four picking. But we've got plenty of blueberries for a while."

He paused, then, "I did just the way my poor single mother did for me and my brother. We were a little younger than Hunter here when she took us to a cotton field in south Alabama to pick cotton for an entire day. Now doing anything for a full day is just about beyond the attention span of twelve- and fourteen-year-olds."

Everyone laughed. They were listening.

Brooks laughed too, then continued. "Gentlemen, I want you to know I made thirty-five cents for a whole day's work. Hard work. Back-breaking work. And then I spent it all at the closest gas station on a Baby Ruth candy bar and a Coke-Cola."

Everyone laughed.

"Just one Coke?"

"Maybe we pooled the remaining pennies and split another one," remembered Brooks.

He shifted and turned toward another section of folks. "Anyway, yesterday at Food World, I noticed that a small carton of blueberries sells for three dollars. That's inflation!"

"You know it."

"So, did my children or me and my brother learn anything about the economy? About running a business? About how much things cost? About labor and wages? Probably not."

"Naw."

"Naw. Young'uns."

Brooks turned again and gestured toward the circle of men. "But *we* know, and they will learn."

"That's right."

Jordan had eased into the room and had taken a seat in his brother's lap. Vincent let him stay. Arlo stood guard between Vincent's legs, wary of the strangers.

Brooks continued speaking to the group. "I respect those who work with their hands and backs in agriculture or manufacturing. In fact, I've never met a farmer who doesn't also work with his head because agriculture is a business. You don't have to go to college like Rory here to be a farmer."

The group laughed.

"And whether you're assembling manufactured homes or growing corn, at the end of the year, after you've paid your bills and your workers and yourself, you know what your profit is."

"That's rite."

"We get paid, too?" Paul asked quizzically.

"Not much," said Elvis.

Brooks continued, "Successful businesses each utilize some form of planning. What seed will cost next spring, how much a new piece of equipment costs, what beef is projected per pound."

"That's why God gave us wintertime. That's when I do all that," said Colt.

"Me, too."

Brooks pulled an empty chair to the center and sat down. He mopped his forehead with his handkerchief. "So, you don't want a poultry-processing plant built uphill from your watermelon fields."

"Nowhere close."

"Nope."

"You don't want a BMX track built next door to your home."

"No way."

"What about a bar or pool hall next to a day care center? Is that ever a good idea?"

"No, sir."

"You don't want clear springs drained dry by a new housing development, do you?"

"Hell, no."

Rory thought about his water problem caused, in part, by the new highway. He asked Brooks what a landowner can do in cases like the ones he mentioned.

Brooks answered, "Land use in unincorporated rural areas is mostly open. Whatever. Counties do a good job regulating, states do good jobs, the utility companies do good jobs being environmentally good citizens. But consider this: the purchaser in a real estate deal does not have to disclose who he is or what he may or may not do."

"Damned foreigners."

"Damned chemical companies."

"We'd tar and feather 'em."

"And that's against the law. The law will protect you if you're incorporated. Then *you* decide what types of businesses can be built near your homes and schools. You collect money …."

"You mean higher taxes," Samuel interrupted rudely.

"I mean revenue to spend on what your voters want most."

"Like what?" he asked.

"A park with swings and a slide perhaps, for the children," answered Brooks. "A library for booklovers and students. A commercial area separate from residences. A nearby retail spot for folks who need to shop."

John spoke up. He said he was against incorporation but did want a traffic light at the crossroads where most traffic accidents take place.

Elvis interrupted, "We ain't a town. Ain't a city. We'uns just a country crossroads with a couple o' mailboxes."

Winston agreed. "You're talking big ideas. We don't want that. Now that only local traffic goes through Littafuchee, we just want to be left alone."

Brooks countered the isolationists' viewpoint.

"Men, you'll never be left alone. The modern four-lane has created prime real estate along both sides of the highway. Littafuchee will grow whether you want it to or not. Why not have a say with a mayor and city council?"

Mr. Ludeke spoke up. He told the group that he'd promised to sell his frontage to Lin's family for the cost of a handicap van so he could get Maudie to her appointments.

He said, "They going to build a *ben zin*, a gas station, with a many of pumps that take credit cards. They build a store with groceries en dairy products. I won't have to go into town to a big grocery store for diapers for Maudie."

A cold silence followed.

Elvis asked, "What about the Negro, Mr. Ben? Is he coming back?"

Mr. Ludeke shifted awkwardly in his chair.

All eyes turned to Vincent for clues. Vincent sat stone-faced, an observer only, but Jordan smiled and nodded his head *yes*. "Maybe mayor," the boy added.

Elvis stood up and left the meeting. He slammed the door shut. Eyes darted and met wide-eyed expressions.

Unaware, Mr. Ben began, "Yep. You see, I've gotten ten good year ahead of me, I figgar. Everett en I gonna be partners, you see. *Jawohi*. We're goin' into the tree farm business. I've got the land and machinery. That boy, er, man, got *klug* lik' a New Orleans lawyer 'n the *gehirn* of a 'lectric countin' machine. I can carry da whole sha-bang for t'ree year 'fore we start rakin' in da dough. En, you see, he's nice company to have livin' in my house. Fixes things for free. *Kostenlos*. So, I'm for incorporating to bring peace, so my workin' pardner don't get shot up like Ms. Carmen."

"Me, too," began Pratt Peterson. "I'm considering selling my dairy barns and converting the migrant camp into a mobile home village. One gits me a retirement fund. Two gits me regular rents coming in for me and Prissy to spend traveling. My frontage along the highway ain't big enough for much, 'cept maybe a self-serve car wash. But rite next to the new modern gas and convenience store, it'll do well. I *am* a businessperson, you see. I know there's money to be made off the land. Can't eat dirt when a person retires."

"You're a sell-out, Peterson! You and the old German both!" shouted Samuel, pointing his finger in his face.

Jaime stood up. Then John.

"Well, I'll eat dirt before I sell," shouted Paul.

"I'll eat dirt before I sell to the Negro," said John.

The meeting grew uncivil.

"Calm down, fellas," said Rory. "This is my home. I have young children here."

"I can't calm down. I'm so gol' dern mad I could chomp nails right now," said Paul, hands and voice trembling.

He continued, "Wait 'til Joe hears your plans, Mr. Pratt. Your frontage is directly across the four-lane highway from his. And Mr. Ben? Foreigners owning a store in Littafuchee just ain't gonna happen. I promise you that over my dead body."

The disgruntled, rambling threats continued.

"Take it outside, men," said Rory firmly. He opened the front door and gestured.

"Gentlemen, this meeting is officially over," said Brooks in a dignified manner. "However, I will hang around to answer any follow-up questions you may have. A petition comes first. Like links in a chain. But I urge you all to go home and think about what you can do to make this a better place for your children and grandchildren. An incorporated Littafuchee will be a safe, beautiful place where there's a formal way to voice dissenting opinions."

About half the men stormed outside in one mass like a flotilla of angry ants surprised by weather conditions beyond their control.

The other half moved to the dining room table like somber jurors to deliberate. They were served coffee and cake by Laurice and Francie who had heard the entire meeting from the kitchen.

Then there was a knock on the door. Were the dissenters returning? Vincent stepped out to get his uncle's pistol.

Francie went to answer the door to find Glenn Howton standing there.

"Hi."

"Hi."

"What's going on here?"

"There's a meeting."

"Can you come outside? Maybe we could go for a walk."

"I'll ask my mother," said Francie, who hadn't seen Glenn since they'd examined the contents of Granny Bea's keepsakes the second time.

She wanted to escape the tedious questions the men were likely to discuss.

Laurice let her leave upon the condition they avoid the men who'd left the meeting armed and angry, which was no problem as they were pulling out, headed to the Feed 'n Seed to brief Mr. Joe.

Laurice liked the boy, Glenn. He was polite and seemed studious, the kind of boy mothers feel safe letting their daughters date.

"Ask him to Sunday lunch, Frances," whispered Laurice as she handed Francie a flashlight.

Francie bounced down the front steps to Glenn who was standing below.

He examined her quizzically, then complimented her. "I like your new glasses."

"I was wondering when you were going to notice. So, you do?" Francie asked. She smiled at him, pleased.

"Yes, most definitely," he said, wearing a quirky expression.

Francie asked, "What's going on?"

He dug into his jeans pocket and retrieved a small white jewelry box. "I have something for you."

"For me?" Francie said, her heart racing.

She opened the box. Inside was the rose quartz arrowhead fashioned by a jeweler into an exquisite pendant necklace on a sterling silver chain.

"It's beautiful, Glenn!"

"I did put a leather strap on it. When my mother saw it, she said it would do if I liked the girl; but it wouldn't do if I loved the girl."

Francie blushed at the thought of him having this confessional with his mother. She remembered feeling threatened when he took it away that day at the springhouse. Now she knew she could trust him.

"I love it. Put it on me."

He did. Then he kissed her neck. It felt soft and warm. She smelled nice. "Let's go for a walk, huh?"

"Sure."

They strolled slowly down the familiar path that led to the springhouse and Talwa Creek. A row of fragrant tea olive shrubs lined the uphill side of the path. The air was intoxicating. Francie broke off a delicate white cluster and put it in Glenn's buttonhole.

Along the way on the other side of the winding path, an old clothesline had been repurposed as a trellis for a cultivated honeysuckle vine. The healthy, deer-resistant vine produced an abundance of pink and yellow Goldflame honeysuckle blooms. During the daytime, Francie's view of the trellis from her desk inside the springhouse was of the iridescent hummingbirds and colorful butterflies drinking the plant's sweet nectar. It was very calming. She felt calm now.

Glenn broke off a cluster and pulled the nectar through the bottom of one tube. He touched it to Francie's lips. The single drop oozed from the tube to her lips in slow-motion. He bent down and kissed her, licking the sweetness off her lips before inserting his tongue, which Francie readily accepted.

They kissed long and passionately for teenagers new to romantic experiences.

He pulled her close to him. This time she relaxed into his embrace. He had told his mother he loved her. She would say it to him tonight.

They strolled closer to Talwa Creek, listening to the rushing stream of water break over rocks along its path. Warm mist swirled from damp earth, filling their path with ethereal beauty.

They stopped in the darkness. Francie turned off the flashlight. It was near pitch black.

Glenn's touch created new sensations in her.

"I love you, Glenn."

"I love you, too," he said, as his hand went under her shirt.

"Can we be together tonight?" he asked. "*Be together*, you know? I brought a condom, just in case."

Francie looked around in the dark. Thick moss and ferns grew down the north side of the tree they stood beside. Its padded roots ran down to the creek. The creek's sounds and the night birds calling was mesmerizing.

"Here. This is perfectly romantic," she said.

"Wait!" he said.

He grabbed an old quilt from the springhouse and spread it on top of the greenery. He eased her onto the quilt and faced her. He removed her ponytail holder and fluffed her hair around her shoulders. It fell in thick dark locks front and back.

"You are so beautiful like this," Glenn whispered. He removed her glasses, carefully folding and tucking them into a crevice. "You take my breath away."

"That's how I feel about you," she replied.

She removed his glasses and tucked them beside hers.

They French kissed some more.

Glenn stood up and removed his polo shirt. It was the first time she'd seen his bare muscular shoulders. He had a small tuft of chest hair.

Only in the Bible Belt would a southern virgin's mind retrieve the image of a young David from the Good Book. Yet, head to toe, his physique was perfectly Davidic. Kingly. Sexy. She knew he wanted her to see him.

From that moment, any sense of time and place evaporated from Francie's attention except how Glenn was making her feel. It was all so new. She felt she was the center of the universe for once.

Glenn, in his matter-of-fact manner, said, "I've never had these kinds of feelings for anyone else. I love who you are, and I want to do everything right by you. You are my soul mate, Francie. I just know it."

He smothered her with tender kisses all over.

Francie's body reacted naturally to their lovemaking. The air in her lungs came out in soft vocalizations that suddenly got louder. She shuddered.

Glenn put his mouth over hers and whispered into it. "Sh-h-h! I know. Sh-h-h, I know."

The couple laughed in whispers. Francie memorized the few minutes it had taken to do a thing profoundly bonding.

They cuddled.

"Why do you like me, Glenn?" she asked. "I'm not beautiful like Kimberlee or some of the other high school girls."

He studied her face, memorizing it.

He said endearingly, "You are my idea of beautiful. You look like a classic painting with your hair loose, wearing the pink necklace I had made for you."

She rubbed the arrowhead in her fingers. It no longer represented Granny Bea's Half-Moon stories of Native Americans but her lover's affection for her.

"Why did you start talking to me in the library?" Francie continued with her questions, which came like lightning to her mind.

"I had to."

"Why?"

"My mother said I had to spend some time with you to see if I liked you."

"Why? I've never met your mother."

"Well, she's Pratt and Prissy Peterson's daughter."

"Really!? He was at the meeting tonight. He didn't seem mean like everyone says."

"He's not. One time Ms. Dovie gave Mother your name and said that you had been the smartest girl in the eighth grade."

"That's not enough to make any boy like me. Probably just the opposite."

"And, that you were the only girl to answer one question correctly. So, we would make a good couple. That's what Ms. Dovie figured."

"I did? Heck! What was the question?"

Glenn knew it instantly. He had asked several girls who were in his calculus class. None of them knew.

"What does an internal combustion engine convert?"

Francie answered quickly, "Chemical energy into kinetic energy. Dad told me about that at the auto show."

"Right. And toxic pollutants into less harmful byproducts."

"When did I pass your test? When did you start liking me of your own accord, like seriously?" she queried.

Glenn was lighthearted in his reply. "Well, pretty much the combustion engine answer. Plus, on that first day, you were reading a forestry magazine. Does a dumb girl do that?"

"Pine beetles," replied Francie. "I was trying to find another solution for our pine beetle infestation than Dad cutting down all his pine trees."

"And," said Glenn with a smile, "that Friday when we were in my car on the way out of the student parking lot. Remember? Liam leaned his head in and stuck his ABC gum into your mouth. You spat it back in his face and shoved him out onto the parking lot."

"… and called him a misogynistic imbecile," Francie finished. "I poured my soda on his crotch, too."

"Yes, you embarrassed him. He hasn't been able to get a date ever since."

"I told some popular girls he peed himself. I told my friends he had bad breath!" Francie laughed, recalling the vindication she got.

Francie was back in her overthinking mode. She said emphatically, "But that doesn't make sense, Glenn."

"Don't take this wrong," began Glenn, "but I wasn't looking for a dolled-up girlfriend who's all clothes and makeup. I wanted someone real and uncomplicated like you."

"That is *not* a compliment," said Francie.

"It is, though," countered Glenn. "See, we can talk about stuff, have intelligent conversations. We laugh at each other's jokes. It's so comfortable with you in the passenger seat beside me."

Francie kissed his chest and let her hand wander.

She teased back, saying, "That's what I like about you. You're straightforward. And you remind me of Dad with your weird jokes. They're funny weird, Glenn. I must figure them out."

Glenn shrugged. "Well, that's a buzzkill. I remind you of your father."

Later, as they started to stroll home together, something stirred in the bushes at the thick tea olive shrubs. They stopped and turned on the flashlight but decided it was squirrels playing chase. They did not see the crouched tattooed figure hiding there.

By this time, the pro-incorporation group was standing in the yard with a few wives listening from the porch with Laurice.

Glenn nodded to Rory and Vincent, then he got in his car and left. Like Wyatt, he was part of the river community. Unlike Wyatt, he knew when not to interfere.

Francie joined the women on the porch, who began teasing her about her new boyfriend.

"You know you're second cousins, right?" asked Ms. Mary.

"I thought it was third cousins," added Ms. Dotty.

Francie smiled, unperturbed. "Oh, you mean like Queen Elizabeth and Prince Phillip?"

The ladies chorused, "Oh-h-h, we didn't know they were cousins, too."

Only Francie's mother noticed her daughter's ponytail was down. With caution flags in her mind, she remembered the power of first love.

CHAPTER 18

Billboard at the Crossroads

Prejudice and bigotry are brought down by the sheer force of determination of individuals to succeed and the refusal of a human being to let prejudice define the parameters of the possible.

—CONDOLEEZZA RICE, FORMER US SECRETARY OF STATE

When most folks encounter a swarm of wasps, they know to either leave it alone or to walk away in the opposite direction. Francie, however, rode her bicycle directly to one and walked in the front door. She was agitated grievously about a hateful billboard atop the Gillivray and Gillery Feed 'n Seed store.

"Who put up that billboard about my dad?" Francie demanded the second she stepped inside the Feed 'n Seed.

"Not enny o' dese fellas," said Buddy while he applied tobacco to Jimbo's face, swollen and red from multiple wasp stings.

Honk.

Francie turned to Opalee who was snickering behind the cash register as she applied an icepack to her father's arms and neck where multiple wasps had gotten to him with their painful stings.

"Did you, Opalee?" Francie demanded louder.

"Naw."

"I know you told the ladies at the Sheer Success that Dad had stolen money from the group trying to incorporate. They told their husbands," Francie said indignantly.

"Prove it."

"They simply opened a bank account to pay bills for things needed," said Francie.

"Needed? Like a kid's sl-i-d-e, I heard," chimed in Opalee.

"A playground, pencil brain."

"Someone said that someone else said that tha other nite at tha meetin' someone gave someone money to buy the huntin' camp property, too."

"Another lie."

"Shure seems to describe your pa, Franc-i-e," retorted Opalee. "A liar and deceiver."

"You are evil, Opalee," said Francie. She turned to Joe Gillery, "Mr. Joe, did you put up that sign?"

"Naw, young 'un," he said.

Honk.

Kimberlee and her grandfather wandered in from the rear loading area with boxes of new goods purchased in Birmingham's wholesale district. The two walked into the middle of the condensed soup of crazy heating up.

"What's going on here?" Houston asked, setting down a box of coffee and creamers on his counter.

Honk.

"Mr. Houston, did you put up that billboard? The one claiming my dad is a murderer and a drug dealer?" asked Francie.

He looked puzzled. "A billboard? Our billboard?"

Houston stepped out the front door and down the steps. He strained to see against the afternoon sun's glare. Aloud, he read the amateur artwork covering the roof's billboard:

> *The devil will git you*
> *if you sign Rory Kirwin's petition.*
> *Don't listen to a likely*
> *drug dealer*
> *a murder suspect*
> *and a nixxer-lover.*
> *You are being tricked by a liar.*
> *Honk if you are against incorporation*

Honk.
Honk.

"Damn it!" the old storekeeper shouted. He spat on the pavement.

Honk.

"Who's responsible for that crap of a sign?" he huffed out loud as he reentered the store. "Joe, did you?"

"Meybe," Mr. Joe replied insolently.

"Opalee wrote it. We just put it up for her," said Bucky.

Mr. Joe pushed his daughter forward to offer her up as the scapegoat.

He said, "Opalee's got a powerful hate for the Kirwins. She swears to go to her grave before Littafuchee incorporates, bringing in darkies and Asians and druggie riffraft. Ya know, she can convince these fellas to do anything. She's got womanly ways. I don't have to say nutin'."

Opalee continued forward until she was within reach of Francie. She went for her face with her fingernails. In doing so, she jerked off Francie's new glasses. She laughed manically as she twisted and folded the frames until they broke.

"Aw-w-w!" screamed Francie.

She drew her fist back and punched Opalee in the nose with such force it made a cracking sound. Blood gushed out. Infuriated, Francie punched her nemesis in the ribs, which crippled the woman with sharp searing pain.

"Cat fight!"

"Cat fight!"

Honk.

Kimberlee grabbed Francie's arm and pulled her toward the front of the store.

She begged, "Oh, Fran-c-i-e! Don't hurt Opalee. You're both supposed to be bri-des-maids at my wed-din' one day-uh."

"Kimberlee! Is there any activity in your brain? She has slandered my father. Think. She put these idiots up to a cruel trick that has consequences. And she broke my prescription glasses," Francie said adamantly. Taking in a deep breath, she seethed, "I've never hated anyone so much."

Honk.

"Oh, Fran-c-i-e! We'll git that sign do-w-n, hon-e-e," said Kimberlee while hugging her best friend. "And I can git Pap to buy you m-o-r-a gla-s-ses."

Opalee, with equal hate and venom in her eyes, grabbed the cast iron poker beside the cold pot belly stove in the middle of the store. She snuck up behind them and swung the poker around with as strong a hit as she could manage with broken ribs. She hit Francie's left shoulder, causing her to spin and fall into one of Houston's minnow vats, turning it over, spilling forty gallons of dank water out onto the store's wooden floor. Francie went crashing down, too.

Houston grabbed Opalee and pulled her away. He shoved her toward Joe.

He said, "Here's your lunatic daughter. Lock her up before she kills someone."

"You're the devil," Joe yelled at his brother.

They began an out-of-shape version of fisticuffs which was mostly shoving, grabbing, and missed swings.

"You egotistical, arrogant SOB," Joe yelled.

Honk.

"You secretive, pathetic s-l-o-b," Houston retorted.

Honk.

Protectively, Kimberlee and Francie stepped in front of Mr. Houston.

Francie said firmly, "You leave him alone. Your porch patrol did exactly as they were told by you. They are nothing more than ignorant, hollow men without *your* directives, not Opalee's. And nobody uses the n-word anymore, Mr. Joe. Have some respect because one day rednecks will be the minority."

With little effort, the four elbow boys restrained both girls and Houston.

Joe, wearing an eerily similar expression as Opalee, said, "That's right, boys, get these girls. Do whatever you want with them."

Then he grabbed Bubba's revolver out of its belted holster and held it under Kimberlee's chin.

He warned, "I've got a notion to blow her pretty brains out, Houston. What you say 'bout that, huh? Bro?"

"Joe," Houston said, trying to speak in a calm voice. "Let her go. You and I can talk this out. Let Kimberlee go. Send those ruffians away. I know the two of us can get to some resolution."

"She's just a no-account girl, you said," Joe retorted.

"She's my beloved granddaughter."

"Seems I remember you saying something like that years ago. Brush it off; you'll forget. 'Things will get better,' I recall you saying," Joe said. "Nutin brought Vonnalee back, my *beloved* daughter, did it?"

Honk.

"Or *my* dog, Eli."

"Oh, that? You still holding on to that grudge?"

"No, brother, I'm holding on to your only granddaughter. Is there a difference?"

he said, pushing the pistol barrel deep into Kimberlee's throat, aiming up toward her chin. "You can git another one."

Kimberlee was crying but motionless.

Tears filled Houston's eyes, "No, Joe. You're right. Vonnalee's death hurts because love is deep and personal. I couldn't deal with it. I know the difference between a dog and a human being. I'm sorry. Forgive my choice of words."

Francie spoke up. "Mr. Joe, keep your sign up. Just let Kimberlee go. My dad won't mind. Who's going to believe a silly old billboard anyway?"

Honk.

Joe did not back down, but his demeanor changed.

He turned to Francie and said, "I want him to hurt. To hurt as bad as I do every single day." He clicked the trigger. "My last memory of her is an ongoing bloody nightmare."

Francie took one step toward him and begged, "Shoot me instead, Mr. Joe. I also love Kimberlee deeply. And I think I remember beautiful Vonnalee."

"Francie!" shouted Kimberlee.

Bucky grabbed Francie with his elbow to her throat as soon as she took that step toward his boss.

He said confidently, "Let's hurt her, Mr. Joe. That'll make Mr. Rory hurt. Maybe change his mind 'bout having the Negro move in. Change his mind 'bout tryin' to change Littafuchee."

Bubba took out his pocketknife and flipped it open. He held it under Francie's chin.

"How's this for sending a message to Mr. Rory?" he said.

He began sawing off Francie's ponytail with his pocketknife blade. He had to pull tight on her hair to get it to cut.

Francie wiggled but could not make a sound as Bucky's arm was choking her. She felt dizzy. Clumps of hair began to fall to the floor.

"Stop it!" shouted Kimberlee bravely, although her own life was more imperiled than Francie's hair being cut. "Uncle Joe, Vonnalee's not here, but I am, and I love y'all." She turned to the dog who continued to lap up minnows and said, "Don't we, Eli?"

With wet paws and fish breath, Eli jumped upon Joe's chest. His tail wagged. He licked Joe's arm.

Joe exhaled, calming himself.

Bubba put out his hand, and Mr. Joe returned his Ruger revolver.

Honk.

Slam went the door.

"You motherfuckers let 'em go, or I'll blow your cocks off shure as I'm standing here," said Aunt Dilly, who'd heard the commotion from her gas station.

When she'd seen the elbow boys absent from their post, she fearlessly came running with her shotgun loaded to check things out.

To Dixie County's residents, she embodied the bad-ass female.

Aunt Dilly was a formidable person about as wide at the hips as a doorway with a strong square face and a set of dentures as ill-fitting as George Washington's. Her long steel-gray hair was swept up into a Pentecostal beehive. Her brown cotton print dress had an abundance of gathers and tucks at the sleeves and waist to hide any woman's figure. Her hands were big and toughened from fifty years of pumping gas for her customers.

Dilly was Houston and Joe's real aunt, nearing eighty years of age. And yet, everybody in Littafuchee moved in step to "Aunt Dilly's" commands.

For each person she represented some fearsome female in their lives—the mean aunt, the cruel stepmother, the hateful neighbor, or the foul-mouth senior citizen— dreaded and mostly avoided. She saw herself performing an unofficial policing role keeping foolish young folks on their toes doing the right thing.

Before any of them had been born, she was a different sort—a shy, acquiescent, self-belittling young wife. She stopped accepting male authority from her counterparts after her husband beat her unconscious in the church parking lot when she was eight months pregnant with their eighth child and none of her brothers-in-Christ intervened.

Honk.

Her pet goat, Bill, was at her side wearing a child's long paisley tie which Aunt Dilly used to restrain him, although not often. He stared down the men with the intimidating side-slanted glare mean goats have. Without a backward glance, he used his hind hooves to buck away the foolish dog, Eli, for whom he had little tolerance.

Eli rolled to the floor but quickly stood. The dog continued to snap at some of the hundreds of shiny minnows that, for a few more minutes of life, flopped like a miniature harvest of fish beaching themselves in search of oxygen during Mobile Bay's jubilee.

The goat gave Bubba the evil slant eye. Bubba handed Aunt Dilly his gun. They released the two teenagers.

Honk.

"Take down that sign. I don't wanna see anything with Clyde Kirwin's kin on it. I despise that two-timing soldier," she said.

Quickly Francie put clues together.

"You're Sweet Potato, aren't you?" she asked.

"Huh? How da hell?"

"I read a couple of his love letters to you when he was in the war, World War I. He addressed you as My Sweet Potato."

"Two-timer," Aunt Dilly repeated. "City slicker wife couldn't sing or play a accordion. But I could. Back in the days when I had more vigor, I could lead two mules hitched to a plow, too. Why not me?"

Francie tried to be sympathetic. "I read that. He said nice things in his letters. He mentioned in his break-up letter that you were too young for him. And you know how war changes folks. You must have returned them all to him at some point; but I'll give them back to you, if you'd like."

"Give 'em or not. You know where I'll be 'til the Lord takes me to His heavenly home," she said and answered. "Pumping gas." Then she added adamantly, "And if heaven ain't like Dixie County, I ain't going there."[5]

Her voice sounded tight, as if filled with regret for what could have been.

There was only a moment's poignancy until she returned to her formidable self. She still held all the men at bay with her loaded shotgun, calling them repeatedly a "sorry lot," among other cusswords.

She added sarcastically, "Bobo and Boohoo deserve prison time for killin' Carmen O'Rourke. She told the truth, that's all. Nobody else's business who she spread her legs for."

Honk.

She commanded Opalee to go across the store to sit beside her mother, Opal.

Opal had continued to shell a pan of cracked pecans throughout the day without a flinch of reaction to the problems. Opalee touched her mother's shoulder. Opal

---

[5] "Dixieland Delight," Hank Williams Jr. "If heaven ain't a lot like Dixie, I don't wanna go; If heaven ain't a lot like Dixie, I'd just as soon stay home. I was one of the chosen few, to be born in Alabam', I'm just alike my daddy's son, I'm proud of who I am …. Hank Williams Jr."

pulled away from her and scooted her rocker closer to the Vonnalee mannequin by the window.

Three times rejected and in much physical pain, Opalee crumpled into a single wad of valueless humanity beside the rocker at the hem of Vonnalee's glistening taffeta ball gown. The discarded daughter with no hope for human comfort could be heard moaning like a quiet, wounded animal.

Honk.

"Git, gals. Over to my station. Now," commanded Aunt Dilly.

They did, with Bill chasing them across McIntosh Road.

Honk.

They entered the dilapidated gas station and hid underneath the dark walnut and glass display case. But before that, Francie called 911.

"Hurry. People have guns out at the Feed 'n Seed in Littafuchee," she said, quickly hanging up and dialing home. "Bea, go get Dad and Vincent now. Fast. Tell them there's a fight at the Feed 'n Seed. We're hiding at Aunt Dilly's."

As she hung up the phone, the teens heard a crash from the store. They looked out to see the goat had used his horns to bust out the plate glass store front to get back inside the store to Dilly. (The mannequin fell into Opal's lap.)

Within seconds, Bill was chasing all four elbow boys outside through the wooden door. This commotion set the rooftop wasps into high alert mode for the second time that day. In military precise formation, they swarmed out of the stove pipe vent. The first moving object was targeted as the major threat and that was the men fleeing the store.

Buddy, Bubba, Bucky, and Jimbo were chased by Bill into the local traffic at the crossroads.

Honk.

"Fools!" a driver shouted.

Head down, horns forward, the mean white and brown goat charged at them. They turned south on the railroad tracks where they ran as fast as they could, tripping on the difficult rails, timbers, and gravel. However, the goat danced lightly along the train tracks like a happy puppy in a game of chase. He pursued them around the big curve before turning back.

The wasp swarm did a ninety-degree turn at the crossroads when a tall utility crane turned into their path. They encircled the Feed 'n Seed building at the gutter line.

Wyatt pulled up beside the store in a Golden Yokes Eggs semi cab truck, pulling his fireworks trailer. His latest idea to get a vote had begun.

Driving up to set down the fireworks trailer on Houston and Joe's private property *unauthorized* was not the most stupid thing Wyatt would do that afternoon. But, it was the last thing he would do in his life.

In her bedroom slippers, Aunt Dilly, the queen of the colony, plodded out onto the front landing and shot the heck out of the elbow boys' odd assortment of kitchen chairs with Bubba's handgun. The chairs were reduced to twisted metal frames and splintered plastic.

As she was swapping out for her shotgun, the wasps were summoned into action again by Wyatt's noisy arrival. Unaware of the triple dangers but eager for a shoot-out with the elbow boys, he ran toward the gun blasts. His last stupid decision was to run up to Aunt Dilly with his Smith and Wesson drawn.

Honk if the mannequin was the only one who felt no pain that day.

Honk.

CHAPTER 19

Tornado Tutorial

The lights began to flicker and eventually go out. Everything for a moment was silent, then the doors began to violently open and close from the pressure. My dad with another guy began to hold the door closed while the tornado raced towards my town. Then the noise of the tornado began while it tore through the houses around the middle school. It sounded like a train rushing right past me. My sister began to bawl, yet I was perfectly calm. I saw my friend cover her head, so I followed suit. A lady from my church put herself over my friend and I and she began to hum "Amazing Grace." I never felt scared, but remember thinking "Am I going to die?"

—Becca Bowman, Sixth Grader, Nov. 17, 2013. Quora.com

- Since 1950, fifty-nine tornadoes have been rated EF5. Weather.com.tornado
- The historic tornado super outbreak of April 27, 2011, killed 240 people. AL.com
- The average occurrence of tornadoes over a thirty-year period in Alabama (1989–2018) is forty-seven per year in all categories (F1-F5). weather.gov.bmx
- The Huntsville area lies in the Tennessee Valley, surrounded by the hills of the Cumberland Plateau. It also lies within Dixie Alley, an area which is prone to violent, long-track tornadoes. www.al.com
- Why do tornadoes not hit big cities? Cities are specks on the map compared with the sprawling rural land surrounding them. Science.howstuffworks.com
- Alabama tornadoes have most frequently occurred in Jefferson, Mobile, and Baldwin Counties. Montgomeryadvertiser.com

CHAPTER 20

Littafuchee Vanished

The original settlers' descendants remind me of a long clothesline of tattered work clothes flapping in the wind, stubbornly independent but held together by the shared clothespins of poverty and illiteracy with tragedy waiting in the dirt below.

—ANNE BEATRICE, AGE FORTY-EIGHT, YEAR 1951

Unannounced, an EF3 tornado touched down in Dixie County on a quiet Sunday morning in September.

Typical for a Sunday, some farmers were returning to their fields and feeding their livestock.

Worshippers filled churches.

Back-to-back freight trains announced their progression through the county in whistle blasts and track rumblings.

Cars and semitrailers sped through on the new four-lane highway creating one kind of background noise while slow farm trucks on the old two-lane created a different noise.

The seventeen-mile-long, half-mile-wide swath of the tornado's path caused catastrophic loss.

First touching down in the industrial area of Ellisville, it leveled wooden buildings and took apart metal structures.

This touchdown happened so quickly that of the towns' many storm shelters, few were occupied. High winds with flying debris caught and killed folks running for shelter as it passed. No civil defense emergency warning was in place in the county yet.

Ahead of the EF3 hitting Littafuchee, Chip Gillivray sped to Harvest Church to warn others. Failing to outrun the funnel, his truck was picked up and dropped several hundred feet away. He sustained a dislocated shoulder, broken hip, and a concussion.

When he came to, he saw the razed rural landscape behind him. It was strewn with animal carcasses and building debris. Telephone and power lines. Broken pine trees and scrub bushes were flattened in a swirled pattern. Large trees broke in place. On a hilltop he saw dilapidated mobile homes flipped and contents emptied. A lone, hunched individual wandered there amid the destruction, confused, trying to find something familiar.

A torrential rainfall had beat down all night at Gillivray and Gillery Feed 'n Seed. It had quieted to an eerie stillness as the funnel plowed steadily toward Littafuchee.

Prior to it reaching the store, Joe Gillery was stocking his shelves with canned meats and paper products. Opal sat unresponsive to his venomous tirades about the new highway and how it would ruin their business. She felt for the sharp sewing scissors hidden in her pocket. One day she would kill him.

He moved into the storage room and slammed Opalee over a desk. She dreaded what he wanted. She had endured molestations ever since Vonnalee won her first beauty contest. She had served as the victimized object for both his lust and his anger. She held onto the desk edge while her father, with an air of entitlement, yanked down her pants. She slid one hand under her magazines for the box blade cutter and with one finger slid the bar on top exposing the razor blade.

He was just beginning when he noticed the walls of the store make an unusual creaking, popping noise. He ignored that sound plus the ensuing fierce shaking of the lapboard exterior walls. He grabbed Opalee's right hand and shook away the weapon.

With a loud snap, the ceiling pulled apart near the building's center line. Old wooden coffins, kept for decades in the attic, fell, spilling their secret vintage contents – white robes and pointed hoods – on top of Ms. Opal.

Then the entire metal roof and underlayment peeled off, swirling like thin paper. It took Opalee with her pants wrapped around her ankles. In that fleeting moment, Opalee regarded herself as free. *Better than here.* She relaxed into the fierce velocity of the wind as it catapulted her skyward. *Better dead than alive here* were her last conscious thoughts.

As if murderous revenge had been released from the coffins, a long piece of splintered wood stabbed deep into Joe's chest. He was lacerated repeatedly by the tines of swirling saw blades and pitch forks falling off the stockroom wall. He yelled for help as the lifeblood seeped from his body. He screamed out in pain, his venom silenced finally along with the pathological hate with which he had contaminated gullible men for decades.

At Harvest Church near the railroad tracks, the roof collapsed. Because it was low, built of concrete blocks, and had small classrooms, all congregants were spared.

Not so lucky were four teenagers sitting together in one Jeep in the church's parking lot listening to loud music. The red safari-style vehicle was lifted horizontally from the ground and spun like a helicopter blade until it caught in power lines. Twisting into the live wires, it fell into a rain-filled ravine. All were electrocuted.

Portions of a CSX freight train were scattered along the tracks like tin cans. Two box cars blocked the local intersection.

Before the tornado reached the Kirwin's barn, which was next in its path, Vincent and Kimberlee were in the barn's hay loft making love for the second time that morning.

Days before they had decided to get pregnant to honor Carmen. Moved by Kim's unusual selflessness, Vincent realized he'd rather be with her than to see the world. She could heal the hole in his heart, she'd assured him.

Cuddling afterward, they paid no attention to Thunder's restlessness or the tack room door slamming open and shut repeatedly.

"I wouldn't be the first preggie hi sko-o-l-er," she explained to him over these noises.

"I'll make you happy, Kim, I promise. You are my everything now."

"I know," she smiled beguilingly just as a yellow butterfly lit on her nose.

Vincent brushed it away. It landed on her breast. He blew it off.

Then abruptly the butterfly flew backward. They sat up and watched the strange occurrence. They realized it wasn't flying but being sucked backward the entire length of the barn, landing with a *splat* against the screening on the loft ventilation.

The soft straw underneath them seemed to shift, dividing into two sections along a fault line in the old structure. They began sliding. His tall frame encased hers for protection.

They heard loud snapping and cracking.

The last things Vincent saw were the barn's timber supports collapsing. The last thing Kimberlee saw was an ominous void through the peeling tin roof. They fell. The heavy cracked timbers and antique items in the attic caved in on top of them.

At Remnant Church across the railroad tracks on Plank Road, Sunday school was just ending. The children were allowed free time within their portable classrooms.

In the fellowship hall, all the adult classes had met together for a testimonial and coffee for their preacher's tenth anniversary.

The kitchen committee ladies, debating the use of mustard or mayonnaise in potato salad, happened to glance from the rear kitchen window to see the dark funnel-shaped massive tornado approaching the church. They ran screaming into the fellowship hall.

The chaos that followed was like a street riot.

Parents ran toward their children's classes.

Deacons directed others down the crowded stairs to the basement.

In the sanctuary, some men began opening windows and doors so the storm could blow through. Others came right behind closing them so the storm would blow over.

Rory thought to turn off the main natural gas line into the brick building.

The screams of the terrified congregants filled the church as the edges of the funnel reached the portable classrooms in the rear. Folks stopped short of going outside, helpless to prevent the unbelievable scene before their eyes.

As the tornado plowed through the portable classrooms, the light metal trailers rolled through the cemetery like matchbox cars, breaking headstones and tossing children of all ages and sizes out like tiny game pieces. Not one or two but dozens.

By the time it passed, the air was saturated with dust and dissonant sounds. Children screamed. Men and women sobbed in anguish. Babies whined and cried pitifully. The lifeless children and teens had landed on the ground in crumpled heaps on top of each other, broken arms and legs entangled, or they draped individually across headstones, bloodied and motionless.

A chorus of activated car horns from the front parking lot sounded annoying but more tolerable than the alive, injured children in pain.

The heartbreaking anguish taking place inside the cemetery area where the portables were scattered was horrendous. Ancestors' markers streamed tears of rain or blood. Mud painted the scene brown. The sky painted it smoke gray. Shock turned the living into a slow-motion scene of helplessness.

Soul-sick Laurice moaned as she gathered in her embrace the bodies of Albert and Jordan.

Francie stumbled into a heap at her mother's side and fainted.

Tears streamed down Rory's face. His shoulders dropped in total defeat. He fell at the feet of his son and nephew. His wife, smothered in her own grief, was unavailable to comfort him.

Rory tilted his head skyward and screamed at God. "What did we do to deserve this?"

Repeatedly he yelled the question. His voice became raspy, then gave out altogether. He collapsed in front of the little boys' bodies.

Francie regained consciousness with her father shaking her. "Where is Little Bea?" he asked anxiously. "Have you seen my daughter?"

The two checked inside her portable classroom, then under it and around. They went from person to person. They went around to the front of the church building where some of the injured were receiving first aid.

One of the kitchen ladies said she saw Trey chasing after Bea. They crossed Plank Road, she recalled.

Francie and her dad looked over into Peterson's vast pasture. They saw her standing on top of the Native American mound.

"She's alive, Francie! She's alive!" Rory called out rasping joyously.

When they got to the Creek Indian mound, the barbed wire fence was down. Bea was unharmed!

She had chased a mother raccoon with babies clinging to her back. They had been frightened from their tree in the cemetery. When Bea saw the raccoon scamper away, she had followed.

When Trey, the preacher's son, saw Bea cross into the pasture, he ran over to rescue her.

What happened next was unexplainable.

Trey told them Bea froze when the bull approached her. She backed up with each snort or stomp the bull made. He ran up and stood between them, ready to hit the bull with a rock. He told Bea to crawl through the fencing and to get up on the steep mound.

When Bea touched the post, the outer fence posts fell like a circle of dominoes. When she moved to the inner fence, the barbed wires seemed to slip off one post and Bea was able to walk through and up the incline.

"Can you explain it, Mr. Rory?" Trey asked.

"No, not right away," he replied.

"The Indian Spirit commanded it to fall," said Bea. "He pushed me up to the top, too."

Rory heaved relief and did not contradict her.

Francie hugged Trey and told him how brave he was to rescue Bea.

"Will you tell my dad?" he asked. "Will you be sure to say I'm not afraid of the beast or him? Just like that."

"Sure, Trey," said Francie.

The girls ran toward Plank Road while Rory and Trey stood ground against the bull charging them.

Ten minutes. That was the length of time for the destruction of Littafuchee.

Every second thereafter was filled with life-saving efforts by the surviving locals who rushed in with blankets and bandages. The County Emergency Response team arrived. EMTs went into action. Most injuries were head and neck, broken bones, and lacerations.

Farm bells rang in the distance, calling for help. Folks went to help them.

Ben Ludeke left to check on Maudie and Lin. He would bring back Vincent to help.

Firetrucks from nearby towns arrived to put out fires.

The four Kirwins shut out all the activity. In shock, they cradled the boys' limp bodies. All they could do to continue breathing was to hug the lifeless souls and each other tightly until a medical investigator and coroner arrived and signed two death certificates.

Then Francie was sent to find Vincent.

As soon as the officials pulled away in their vehicles with the bodies, Rory turned stoically to the living. Laurice rendered medical help to those with minor injuries.

At the crossroads Mr. Houston sat on the concrete steps outside the skeletal remains of what had been the Feed 'n Seed.

On the parking lot pavement was a line of sheet-covered bodies.

Paul, one of the elderly men at the incorporation meeting, went from body to body praying fervently.

Ms. Dovie consoled and prayed with the grief-stricken survivors.

Houston knew his brother, sister-in-law, and niece were among the shrouded. Joe, at six-feet-four, was the longest mummy shape. The two beside him were the size of children.

He realized he was to blame, in part, for creating the monster his youngest brother was. Instead of making amends, he was guilty of re-creating the dead dog situation throughout their lives. He was guilty of not consoling them when Vonnalee got killed or at any time thereafter. Theirs had been an antagonistic relationship that withheld love and denied death.

He held his head in his hands. *Now it's too late,* he thought. At fifty-eight, he realized he could not replace his brother.

A cold sweat formed all over his skin and crept up from his toes to his stomach before the gastric vomit sprayed out. Forever forward, his stomach would bleed regret.

A television reporter bypassed Houston and the puddle of puke. She went to Paul and had the cameraman get a long shot of the covered bodies and a close-up of the old man praying on his knees.

When she stuck the microphone in his face and asked what he was doing, the scrubby, denture-less old man wearing pajamas and galoshes told her that he had come down to the crossroads to pray the dear souls of his neighbors into heaven.

When she inquired about damage done at his homestead, the old farmer teared up.

Paul's voice wavered, "My home and barn is gone. The chickens is dead, feathers scattered like foxes been at 'em." He spat dip onto the pavement, then concluded, "Lady, I ain't even got a outhouse no more."

That night, neither the line of corpses nor the praying part was used on national news. Only a short clip aired with the lifelong resident of a community that had vanished off the face of the earth, saying woefully, "I ain't even got a outhouse no more."

CHAPTER 21

Holy Ground and Ancestral Spirits

*The land is not ours. Our children are not us. Our integrity is
what we can claim as our only true possession.*

—ANNE BEATRICE, AGE NINETEEN, YEAR 1922, HALF-MOON SHORT STORIES

An hour before dark, Rory returned from across the divided four-lane where he had been working tirelessly with others to retrieve Vincent's body where the search and recovery dogs indicated he was.

Every able-bodied man had pitched in to remove the once grand old barn timber by timber, board by board.

The coroner speculated that Vincent had died instantly sometime within those ten minutes of hell.

Francie, Laurice, and Bea had been watching recovery efforts from their side of Talwa Creek. Francie felt the irony of the swollen creek running full of water over to the other side of the four-lane where they now had no barn, no horses, and no cows.

When Rory reached them, the Kirwins held each other again as a tight family unit so overwhelmed with sadness that the waves of hopelessness crashed into their consciousness repeatedly.

Vincent was dead, too. Kimberlee was clinging to life.

At the springhouse, Rory stopped to stare at where it had been because it was gone. The outbuilding that had stood for over one hundred years and served many purposes had vanished. Its former location was discernable only by the hard-packed dirt floor and the concrete box that protected the clear water used by generations to drink, wash, and chill foods.

Empty glass canning jars had smashed into rock boulders and settled like fragments of cheap sparkling rhinestones at the creek's edge.

From head height to treetop, the pines on Arrowhead Mountain were snapped off like kindling. Hardwoods were stripped of top branches. Four-by-eight sheets of corrugated tin roofing twisted around limbs like bread twist ties. Window drapes, screen wire, and bedding hung from ragged trees like garland. A full mattress. The ugly Turkish rug. A bicycle.

Easily the tornado had lifted the rusted wringer washer and the heavy generator and dropped them several hundred feet up the creek.

Francie saw that the IBM typewriter that Auntie Carmen had given her rested in a niche in a big boulder uphill. The casing was missing. The ink ribbon fluttered from its ribbed guts.

That visual created the realization of a greater, irreplaceable loss. All Granny Bea's writings had been blown away in the tornado.

She scanned the creek, the hillside, and trees for notebooks or sheets of paper. For photographs. Sheet music. For blue ribbons. The decorated boxes of typed stories and the old leather trunk of keepsakes were nowhere to be seen.

Francie remembered Auntie Carmen's song lyrics and cookie tin filled with arrowheads loose in a cardboard box. Gone.

Everything Vincent had turned over to her for safekeeping had vanished like ghosts in daylight.

Turning to her sister, Francie asked rhetorically, "Did you know that your namesake used to write stories about fairies and gnomes when she was a little girl like you?

"She did?"

"She never got to go to Ireland. She wanted to go very much."

Bea smiled, "That's where fairies and gnomes live, right?"

"And sometimes on the cottage roof. Remember Auntie Carmen's bedtime stories?"

Bea nodded yes.

Francie rubbed the pink quartz arrowhead pendant around her neck. For the memory keeper, it was the only keepsake remaining in her possession. An act of God had returned to field and stream the other arrowheads. Auntie Carmen's song lyrics roamed in wisps from ravaged Arrowhead Mountain.

She would never know the pink arrowhead's full story. More than one girl had worn it close to her heart. It had brought more than one girl beauty and belonging, she was sure of that. Right now, it gave Francie a feeling of peace and being loved in this time of terrible tragedy. It would always remind her of Auntie Carmen and Granny Bea.

She turned to Bea and said, "If Granny Bea could be anyone in the world of any time, she'd have wanted to be an Indian princess from one of the Muskogee tribes of Alabama.

"Why?"

"Because they owned the land beneath our feet before we ever arrived in North America."

Francie lapsed into her near-perfect recall. "Princess Half-Moon wanted to see what was beyond the mountain in all directions, especially where the hunters said a broad river flowed with such urgency that it rarely slowed and never stopped."

"What?"

"Granny Bea wrote that," Francie explained. "In her Half-Moon stories."

She turned to her mother, "Mama, did you know Poppa knew how to make moonshine? He used to go to a cave to drink it with other folks."

"Why a cave?"

"Well, the Native Americans discovered the cave first. Then later, there was this thing called Prohibition."

"Oh, yes. That was way before our time."

Rory had begun to listen to Francie, although he kept glancing impatiently up toward the cottage.

She continued, "Before that, Granny Bea's brother invented something that had to do with hydroelectric power. Or maybe it was after Prohibition. And another brother, a chemist from Sheffield, helped invent vinyl siding for houses."

"I did not know that. I was too busy working the farm to listen to Mother's stories," Rory stated regretfully. "I don't remember names very well either, so I can't help you."

Francie turned to her mother. "This is interesting about Granny Bea."

"What's that?" asked Laurice.

"Well, how about this. Like you, Granny Bea didn't like living here when she first arrived in 1927."

"Francie! How would you know something that personal?"

"She told me. In her journal," replied Francie. "I wish Bea could have read her stuff. Seen the very old photographs."

"Little Bea was a baby when her grandmother passed away. She probably doesn't even remember how Dixie County looked before Arrowhead Mountain was blasted in half."

Francie began to quote what prose she could recall.

"Granny Bea wrote that it was 'wide pastoral valleys between scenic mountain ranges dressed in magnificent fall colors, ridges rolling one after the other into the distance, so vast I am drawn into a spiritual high by the beauty of it all.'"

"That's beautiful, Ponytail, e-e-r-r Frances," said Rory. "Thank you for that." He got out his handkerchief.

"She hiked almost every mountain in Dixie County with her hiking club. She got other teachers to go, too. She liked picnics on mountaintops," said Francie.

She continued. "I don't think teachers are supposed to, but she had favorites. Students, I mean. Mr. Houston was one. And some twins she tutored at home. She taught all the sisters in this one family of all girls. She wrote how thoughtful they were to her after they grew up."

"She stopped writing in her journal before she got old, so there's nothing about me and you, Bea. But we can remember for her. Our time with your grandmother."

"Yours, too, Frances," Rory added. "She loved you like you were her bloodline."

Bea asked innocently, "What do folks remember about children after they die?"

"What do you remember about your little brother?" her mother asked, holding back tears but curious.

Bea thought for a moment, then answered, "That he smelled good. And the way his waves stuck against his head when he woke from naps."

"Me, too."

"Me, too."

"Me, too."

Bea said, "My heart smiled every time he called me Wittle Wee."

"My heart smiled every time he stomped his foot. I saw myself," said Rory.

"Or gave his fried okra to Arlo under the table."

"Me, too."

The living stood in silence with streams of tears flowing for the deceased, old and young.

No birds chirped. No hummingbirds darted about. No chipmunks or lizards scampered across the leaves. Bugs were nowhere to be seen or heard.

It was as if all nature had folded in on itself to recover.

At length, her voice choked with pain, Laurice answered, "We'll remember their innocence. The children. We'll remember their goodness. Our kin."

Francie grasped the profundity of what was lost forever. Not trinkets, not journals. It would be the casual interaction of family members supporting each other, day to day.

"Someone should write about all of them," Laurice suggested, hugging her living children. Still, she felt the phantom tug of Baby Bama at her waist.

Immersed in shared grief, Francie clung to her parents for strength. She would not realize for many years that she would be the one to write down what she remembered for the others.

In time, Rory released his embrace of his wife and daughters to walk slowly the narrow uphill path to the empty cottage.

At Laurice's signal, the girls let him go alone.

He found Arlo sprawled listless on the front porch like a lost pup in search of a kindhearted human to take him in.

Rory patted the dog's underbelly and checked him for injuries. He arose and followed his third master inside.

Rory closed the door to shut out everyone else.

A tall pine tree had fallen across the right side of the cottage, sheering off that side of it. The stone chimney had collapsed.

Soot covered the interior objects in a thick gray film.

Discernable by its shape was the leather family Bible on the end table. Inside its pages, scrawled in fading fountain pen ink, he read the marriage, birth, and death entries going back to 1844. He would update it when he found the strength.

Rory strummed Carmen's sooty guitar on the bed where Vincent or Jordan had been playing it. His family's musical talents lingered in his auditory memory.

Vincent's shoes were in alignment beside the waterbed. Jordan's Superman pajamas, now gray and powdery, lay on the worn rug where he had changed out of them that morning.

Rory picked up his nephew's pajamas, slowly folded them, and tucked the bundle inside his own shirt. He grasped his chest, moaning in anguish.

Mentally and physically exhausted, Rory surrendered his form to his sister's rocker, which had been crafted by an earlier generation's furniture maker.

He breathed in pine tar smells of the ancient fires of his ancestors that permeated the chimney, paneled walls, and the floor.

He began to sing softly,

> "When peace, like a river attendeth my way,
> When sorrows like sea billows roll;
> Whatever my lot, Thou hast taught me to say,
> "It is well, it is well with my soul."

> "Though Satan should buffet, Tho' trials should come,
> Let this blest assurance control,
> That Christ has regarded my helpless estate,
> And hath shed His own blood for my soul." [6]

Each time he sang the chorus, he heard Little Bea from the front porch sing the echo.

He could not stop the cavalcade of an unorganized, relentless life review of all those he had loved and now missed achingly.

Rory became the receptacle of their whispered wisdom that life on earth is a sequence of good and tough times. And that death comes to all inevitably. Loving deeply is both the reward and the source of pain for lives intermeshed.

He felt the air charged with their lingering ancient prayers as their spiritual energy poured out over sick children, military relatives serving in wars, for major sinners, and minor transgressors. He felt the energy of forty years' worth of prayers and petitions for *him* that had come from inside the cottage.

In the end, he embodied the countenance of an elder. Spiritually mature. Transformed by his dark night of the soul.

Rory Kirwin chose to embrace God's grace over bitterness. Jesus's example won over Satan's mind games.

While their father was inside the cottage, Francie and Bea sat on the porch steps outside.

---

[6] "It Is Well With My Soul," Lyrics: 1887 Horatio Spafford. Music: Phillip P. Bliss.

Bea said to her big sister, "There's an old man sitting in that porch rocker."

Francie turned but saw no one. She asked her sister what he looked like.

"I dun-no. Old. Nice. Mostly invisible," Bea said. "He doesn't want us to go inside just yet."

"Yeah?"

"He said to me, 'Claim your gifts, child of mine.'"

"Sure."

Bea continued, "I'm to tell Daddy that it's time for us to move on from this land like the Native Americans had to do. Leave it for the new people."

"Like whom?"

"I dun-no," she shrugged. Then picking up at the chorus, she sang the echo in her pure innocent voice, "It is well with my soul."

Francie realized Beatrice would continue Carmen's musical talents. She would carry on her gift alone or with Dad.

When Rory forced the damaged front door open, he saw his girls waiting. They embraced.

Francie asked, "You okay, Dad? We didn't think you'd ever come out."

Their father was visibly shaken and unsteady. They locked arms with him and set out for home in the darkness.

Rory stated flatly, "We are the last Kirwins to live on this land. It's time for us to move on and make room for new people to live here."

Francie looked at Bea with astonishment. Almost verbatim the apparition's message.

"God." Bea smiled her sweetest.

She then explained to the other two. "An angel caught Albert and Jordan. They were always protected inside his wings while the tornado broke everything."

Rory picked up and carried Bea the rest of the way to their house.

"Daddy," she whispered into his ear. "The boys like heaven more than here. More than us. And Vincent is with them."

They found Laurice in Albert's bedroom. A tree branch had punched a wide hole in the ceiling. Rain had soaked everything.

"Come on, Laurice," said Rory softly.

She remained rocking Albert's teddy bear. "I remember Mama Bea telling me once that when she held her lifeless infant son, she thought her life was over. She didn't want to live anymore."

"Her firstborn," Rory replied.

"She went on to live a full life though. She helped so many individuals and students. She made a difference. What if we hadn't had her?"

"Well, I wouldn't be here, for one," said Rory.

"No, not that. I can keep on, too. She can continue to be my role-model. I can carry this suffering, *and* I can do good things too."

She leaned into Rory's embrace. He held her.

Other trees had uprooted and fallen across their long ranch house.

Rory decided the safest place to sleep for the night was in the bed of his dad's old truck parked in a separate shed. He grabbed Spam and crackers from the tumbled pantry items and a jug of orange juice from the broken refrigerator. Laurice gathered the driest blankets and pillows.

Arlo was invited onto the makeshift bed. He draped himself across the girls' legs. His pack had become smaller. He would not fail them.

They consumed the sparse meal speaking little. The parents kissed their girls good night. Rory hummed a familiar tune to lull them to sleep.

Francie felt herself drifting off to that place on the other side of sleep where either magical childhood adventures or hideous nightmares reside. There she would begin to process the day's tragedies.

The Kirwin adults felt burdened with the details awaiting them at daylight.

Silently, Laurice wondered how to plan three funerals.

Silently, Rory wondered how to pay for three funerals without burial insurance.

In time, they slept.

Suddenly, Francie was aware of a presence and opened her eyes to see a foggy mass, more like a breeze with mass, move around the truck bed.

She looked around. No one else stirred except Arlo. His ears perked up. His eyes followed the something.

The dog jumped out of the family bed wagging his tail. He beelined to the children's climbing tree where he looked up into its shredded canopy.

Francie slipped out, too.

By moonlight she followed the dog to the climbing tree. It had been uprooted. The huge three-hundred-year-old oak tree leaned in the direction of the wind's path at about a thirty-degree angle.

Francie could read the names of generations of children and sweethearts, their initials carved deep into the trunk and branches.

She planted her bare feet into the soil and wrapped her thin arms around the rough oak trunk. She wept, hugging their climbing tree - merely a sapling during colonization. A part of their favorite multi-generational family stories, fallen. And yet, Arrowhead Mountain, that monument to geological beginnings, stood as a reminder to her that we are not first, only, or always the owners of the land beneath our feet.

Their history and beauty would be carried forward in fading whispers only for a short time as old-timers moved on and until new families moved in.

Rory pulled Francie away. They sat close together against the damp root ball.

Rory felt the pain of being uprooted but also financial relief, knowing the land would provide generously for them even after it was sold to developers.

Francie could see that her carefree childhood was behind her. She would rely on her resilience to help her family face a changing future. She knew Glenn would be part of it.

Faithfully throughout the night, Arlo kept searching the tree branches for the other children.

The supernatural presence continued to hover over them unnoticed, except for Little Bea who felt it lingering for days.

Morning, mourning, and moving forward faced the Kirwin family of four at daybreak.

The end

- What are a few of your rural experiences of deep meaning?
- Do you recognize the Native American names of counties, towns, and bodies of water near you?
- What is the symbolism of Arrowhead Mountain's cutaways?
- What is the symbolism of the climbing tree?
- What are some cultural and physical barriers to change? Which of these is Alabama continuing to deal with?
- Pros and cons of the generational family unit.
- What is the symbolism of Francie's eye injury, possible blindness, and eyeglasses?
- Was there an Auntie Carmen in your life? Name all her skills. Name all the items in Carmen's apron pockets.
- Each of the young children contributes uniquely to the family. How so? Which child's personality was like yours?
- Were Anne Beatrice and her fellow educators the first catalyst for change in Littafuchee? How?
- Did Laurice contribute to change or was she trapped?
- How are Francie and Kimberlee alike? Different?
- Were Francie and Kimberlee too young for sex? Which one used sex? What all did Glenn do right to court Francie? Would you want your daughter at age fifteen to enter a long-term relationship?
- How were Rory and Carmen alike? What actors would you cast in their roles?
- Were the author's attempts to make you hear the music successful?
- Women who were raised in the South knew females like Opalee. Do you hate or pity her? Why?

- Why does the writer give Laurice the occupation of traveling nurse? Is her point of view important?
- How many ways did Ms. Dovie play significant roles?
- What is the difference between open and closed Communion? Have you ever attended a church like Remnant Church?
- Was the pastor's son, Trey, the token gay in the story? Was he the only one in Littafuchee? Dixie County? What point was the author making through the ladies at Shear Success Beauty Emporium?
- In chapter 17, what do the vehicle "honks" represent? How many were there? Would this attempt to incorporate be successful?
- Why does Wyatt Hugg not fit into any situation?
- What are the elbow boys defending? What else do they do?
- Do you know a "badass" like Aunt Dilly? Did she die in the shootout with Wyatt?
- How many characters have names of Alabama counties?
- How many characters have names of Alabama towns or cities?
- How many scenic points of interest mentioned specifically in the story have you visited?
- When was the last time you read a roadside historical marker?
- Name all the Alabama counties through which Interstate 65 traverses.
- Which interstates roughly follow the Old Federal Road?
- What modern cities does the Old Spanish Trail pass through?
- What is the newest interstate in Alabama?
- What Native American tribes lived in Alabama?
- Have you ever found an arrowhead? Where?
- Do you know someone who has an Indian mound on their property?
- How many Indian mounds still exist today?
- Read aloud your favorite descriptive passage.
- Read aloud your favorite funny passage. Why?